Praise for

THE GEOGRAPHY OF FIRST KISSES

"*The Geography of First Kisses* maps a lush world of love, loss, and memory. Prismatic and crystalline, Davidson's prose dazzles."

—C. Morgan Babst, author of *The Floating World*

"Karin Cecile Davidson's debut story collection, *The Geography of First Kisses*, lives up to the promise of its title, as it transports readers into the lushness of landscapes which range from the Louisiana bayous to the Iowa plains, as each story immerses us in place and is steeped in the longings and yearnings of the human heart. Like the desire of the characters themselves, Davidson's prose crackles on the page, with lyricism that feels effortless. These are stories that linger, and Davidson's stylistic skills, like the characters she so beautifully renders, will leave readers breathless, eager for more."

—Laurie Foos, author of *Ex Utero* and *The Blue Girl*

"Reading *The Geography of First Kisses* is a heady, gloriously excessive experience. Davidson's image-rich prose is succulent, her sensibility generous, and though these stories roam between the South and the Midwest, they're imbued with the deceptively languorous spirit of a Louisiana afternoon in the height of summer."

—Holly Goddard Jones, author of *Antipodes: Stories* and *The Salt Line*

"*The Geography of First Kisses* is a dreamy map of love, longing, and lust. It hums and spins in the fever of the bayous, the flight paths of Ohio, unkempt hotel rooms, flickering drive-ins. Karin Cecile Davidson is a wizard at conjuring bodies let loose on this earth. Reading this book is like discovering a long-lost photo album of old loves."

—Reif Larsen, author of *The Selected Works of T.S. Spivet* and *I Am Radar*

"If you follow the Street of Longing to where it dead-ends, inevitably, at the Avenue of Loneliness, there you will find Karin Cecile Davidson's story collection *The Geography of First Kisses*. These characters long for everything: to be seen fully and to disappear; for this kiss to be the first, for this kiss to be the last; to go far away from this place and moment, to stay right here forever. And so it is for the reader also: I wished these stories never to end."

   —Lori Ostlund, author of *After the Parade* and *The Bigness of the World*

"Whether they're catching minnows by hand or releasing birds back into the wild, the unforgettable characters of *The Geography of First Kisses* navigate landscapes we know and love and fear. Here are stories that astonish, at once fantastic and familiar, told in voices both intimate and enchanting. A resonant collection of vibrant gems!"

   —David James Poissant, author of *Lake Life* and *The Heaven of Animals*

"Each of the stories of *The Geography of First Kisses* pulls the reader into a convincing, nuanced world. And Davidson then manages to exit each story with a particular image in which the emotion—be it glad, resolute, or sad—fits that story's particular protagonist. Kudos!"

   —Joe Taylor, author of *The Theoretics of Love* and *Bad Form*

ALSO BY KARIN CECILE DAVIDSON

Sybelia Drive

THE GEOGRAPHY

OF

FIRST KISSES

THE GEOGRAPHY

OF

FIRST KISSES

* * *

stories

KARIN CECILE DAVIDSON

Kallisto Gaia Press Inc.
1801 E. 51st Street
Suite 365-246
Austin TX 78723
info@kallistogaiapress.org
(254) 654-7205

These stories first appeared, sometimes in different form, in the following literary magazines, with grateful acknowledgment to their editors: "The Geography of First Kisses," winner of the Orlando Prize for Short Fiction, in *The Los Angeles Review;* "We Are Here Because of A Horse," winner of the Waasmode Short Fiction Prize, in *Passages North*; "Skylight" in New Delta Review; "The Biker and the Girl" as "No Better than Distance," finalist for the Matt Clark Fiction Prize, in *New Delta Review;* "Eliza, in the Event of a Hurricane" in *Newfound Journal;* "One Night, One Afternoon, Sooner or Later" in *Gris-Gris Literary Journal;* "Sweet Iowa" in *Story Magazine;* "That Bitter Scent" in *Prime Number;* "Gorilla" in *Animal Literary Review;* "The Last I Saw Mitsou" in *Post Road Magazine;* "In the Great Wide" in *The Massachusetts Review;* "Soon the First Star" in *Filigree Literary Journal;* "If You Ask Them Nicely" in *Saw Palm: Florida Literature and Art;* and "Bobwhite" in *Five Points.*

EDITION, April 2023

ISBN: 978-1-952224-25-6

Cover Design & Illustration: Annie Russell

Author Photo: Angela Liu

www.kallistogaiapress.org

Kallisto Gaia Press books are distributed by Ingram.

In memory of Aunt Lee

—who taught me direction and awe, how to look up at constellations
and down at prairie asters, sea glass, moon snails

And in honor of Nancy Zafris, Lee K. Abbott, Wayne Brown, and Mark Fabiano

—my teachers and fellow writers, gone now, but forever compass points

Pull the curtains back and look outside

Somebody somewhere I don't know

Come on now child, we're gonna go for a ride

—LUCINDA WILLIAMS,

"Car Wheels on a Gravel Road"

CONTENTS

THE GEOGRAPHY

OF

FIRST KISSES

THE GEOGRAPHY OF FIRST KISSES

Compass Points

The first was Leon. **A small, muscular boy.** A midshipman at the academy. He knew about compasses, easterly winds, how to bring the boat about on white-capped seas. I went for his blond hair and his deep voice, both like honeycomb, thick and golden and crowded, the waxen chambers, the echo in my chest.

Summer grew brighter, and I refused to go back home to New Orleans, nearly sixteen, without that first kiss. *Sweet sixteen and never been.* We never said it aloud. Those of us who stayed in the corners at dances, at our own tables. All girls, all the time, not too shy, but not quite pretty enough.

For the month of August, I was away from that southerly place, where algebra notebooks got left behind and streetcars rumbled past and boys sat on the cafeteria steps, smoking because they could get away with it, and girls sat by them, the kind of girl I wanted to be. In that northerly summer spot called Castine, where the great aunts played games of Hearts and Gin in the afternoon, where the berries were small and bright blue, where the beaches were covered with rocks and sea glass and broken pottery, the rules seemed different. I dared myself to walk near the academy and its giant ship, moored by the town's public dock, and when I did, the boys appeared. And then, even when I returned home, they kept appearing.

Leon with his bright curls. He had an arrow in his glance and shot me through the heart. My heart had room for so many more arrows. Little did I know.

Geoffrey with his roaming hands. Small, sweet hands that liked to untie

1

things. Apron strings, kerchiefs, the little gold clasp that held on my bikini top. His eyes were dark pieces of eight that blinked hard, sizing me up and then down, putting me in my place. "You baby," he'd say, reaching out to pinch me.

Buzz with a laugh that broke apart the stars. He liked to drink and do it in his car. He took me to drive-ins and ordered iced cokes in paper cups that he laced with Jack. The smell of whisky on his breath and his breath against my neck. The only film I remembered half-seeing was *Lipstick*, Margaux Hemingway looking down and me looking up through the strands of Buzz's long hair, the vinyl seat pressed against my bare back, the twist of double-braid lashing around my ankles.

North

On the beach of rocks and glass and pottery shards, Leon's hand in mine, I walked away from hair ribbons and shy smiles. He kissed me just around the bend from the gray house where the great aunts lived. I leaned against the splintering bulwark and felt his mouth on mine, warm and suprising, and closed my eyes. The weather was gray and coastal, like the great aunts' house, like a cool hand on the back of your neck, but over Leon's shoulder, when I opened my eyes again, the hills were blue and red, and I felt distracted. Robert Lowell had once lived in the house just above the bulwark and I could feel his lingering presence, in the crooked shutters and pale, weathered shingles, all coming apart and tumbling down the hill like so much poetry. And then a seagull went for us, two blonde heads too close to her nest in the tall lilac spikes of untended lupine. She drove us down the beach just in time to save us from the rising tide.

Leon's letters arrived in the same way that the seagull's young must have, too late in the season and demanding unimaginable things. I spread the pages over the flowered spread of my twin bed, so unlike the pale white coverlets in Castine, and read words like *trace* and *lips* and *undone*. Embarrassed, I put the letters away in the bedside drawer where later my mother would discover them. She said she didn't read them, but I wouldn't have cared if she did.

Around the edges of the lake, where bleached oyster shells were heaped, the metallic breeze carried traces of brackish water, diesel fuel, rubber boots. I had turned sixteen, saved from being all too sweet, but still sweet enough. I thought about sailing alone, then decided to sit on the shore and watch the shrimp trawlers head out, the dusk pink and violet and falling around them like the shellfish they'd soon catch. Leon was up north in that summer place where the sky was thinner, hued with blue-gray lines, and the sea carried the musk of gulls and lobster traps. For him, the summer place had become year-round. That autumn he wrote his letters, describing in slanted lines how he stood on the bridge of the training ship, still moored, going nowhere until spring, and through field glasses he looked out to the beach where we'd kissed, the gray house a smudge on the horizon.

South

The official end of summer and school a month in, I arrived at a friend's birthday party too early, and the boy hosting it opened his front door in cut-offs and bare feet. A boy from the cafeteria steps, a boy with hands that gestured and lips that curved. He smiled and invited me in to a windowed room, where the floor was wooden and covered with record albums. He asked me to choose one and put it on the stereo. He went to change into jeans, another shirt, and I chose *Blue*. Joni's voice headed into the slow evening like smoke and envy and wishing. When he came back, I realized not only was I early but that it was his birthday too. I had only one gift, but he said he didn't need anything, that my choice in music was enough.

The days grew shorter, but our shadows never seemed to diminish. The birthday boy with hands and lips and approving nods in my direction—due south—walked under the eaves between classes. And during classes. Simply leaving the building in the middle of biology, his dissection kit untouched, his partner unfazed. He bent the rules and I wished I could do the same. I noticed him more and more and stared at him out the window of our geometry class. Mr. Lê Lâm Trung chanted obtuse and isosceles in Vietnamese-French intonations and seemed not to notice my inattention.

Swimming and sailing on hold, Christmas crept in and then came the debutantes and their dates. I thought of Leon, how strange this would seem to him. How he was buried in maritime studies, while I could barely fathom the inner life of a mollusk, the pearly insides so slippery and revealing. Did he count the days until summer? Did he counterweight the months by imagining his bed covered with more than a cotton sheet, a few wool blankets? Did he walk down to the shore, now covered with snow, and wonder where the baby gulls had flown?

East

"Reveal more," Geoffrey said. He sat behind me in homeroom. My last name began with V, his with W. He pulled a barrette out of my hair one morning. I found it later, on the floor in front of my locker with a curl of white paper in its teeth. In blue ink, two words—*your shoulders*. Once we kissed in a closet under the stairs where chemistry supplies were stored, the crushed box of glass beakers, Bunsen burners, and scales the only hint we'd been there. And a sweatshirt on the floor. Really, it was more than a kiss.

Out on Lake Pontchartrain, moving slowly to Lake Borgne, the shrimp trawlers pushed the blue-brown water apart. The seawall—barely a wall, more like a concrete staircase—led down into the water, rather than up. I stood on the top step and considered entering the lake, but it was February and far too cold. Instead, I walked along the rise, marked by topographical city maps as below sea level and somehow stretching even with the horizon. I wondered if Mr. Lê Lâm Trung had anyone out there, an uncle or a brother who searched for shrimp and threw back the bycatch of shimmering little crabs and baby bluefins. Someone who had lasted the trip from Vietnam to Thailand, who had traded the boat crowded with countrymen for one covered in nets bursting with pinks and browns and reds. Someone who each day spied the battered docks and ancient cypress trees of Shell Beach and maybe even stroked the bright black hair of a son born here, in this place of Assumption and Lafourche, bayous all around.

Sometimes when the sun rose, it had a dirty color, like oyster shells lining a parking lot, like pottery pieces littering a northern beach. Other times I slept and didn't see how the colors reached, rose-gold and rich, desperate to find a ceiling or a way out. I'd bury my head beneath my pillow, wishing the morning would disappear. And then I'd be late for school.

The streetcar swayed along its tracks, and I leaned against the closed window and tried to read *Romeo and Juliet*. Inside, beyond the row of wooden benches, the smell of sulfur and dirty sneakers, the driver sang the blues. Outside, standing up, pedaling a bicycle too small for his long legs, birthday boy spotted me. He tried to keep up, pedaling faster, and then rode past. Way ahead. His hair, like mine, was straight and shoulder-length and flew out behind him. I knew he'd seen me watching him. He played basketball and dated cheerleaders. Girls who, aside from yelling and bouncing at afterschool games, were pretty and elusive, who didn't seem to see him at all. I made this up, this not seeing him part. I imagined they saw plenty of him. Arm in arm, hull to hull.

Spring raced in with wild colors. Azaleas of pink and lilac, red and white, lacey and bright and reaching, outside front porches and in the park. In front of our apartment building there were only hedges, dark green and tinged with dirt. For Mother's Day I went for flowers and ended up with a small bubble-shaped terrarium. My mother thought it sweet and just her style—no maintenance, a miniature ecosystem that would take care of itself. Until it didn't. Rabbit tracks and moss and a small clump of maidenhair fern were the only plants that survived. The curved sides of the bubble encouraged condensation, drops cascading over greenery, and I thought of emerald and teal prom dresses caught in a downpour.

West

The phone rang and Buzz was on the other end. Talking dirty into the receiver. In English class he'd had some ideas about Shakespeare that our teacher, Mrs. Newell, didn't appreciate. Not embarrassed by words like *fuck* anymore, I listened with interest. He wanted to take me to the drive-in and peel off my panties. I wanted to let him. I wanted to hear a car radio, maybe his, so that it sounded like the inside of my mind, crazy and careless and not quite right. One of Lowell's love-cars might pull up and parallel park next to my desire. The moon would surely refuse to shine.

In World History class Mr. Ferdinandez peered through his glasses at all of us. He had wide eyes and black brows and white short-sleeved shirts. At lunch he'd play chess with the freshman boys. But in second period he leaned over his desk and told us about Catherine the Great and her penchant for stallions. We'd made our way through Eastern Europe into Russia, and before I even considered the horses, I thought of the word *penchant*. The liking, the longing, the wishing, the preference for dark hooves and fetlocks, the stretch of the cannon widening up into the hock, the shuddering stifle, and the warm dusty, grassy air all around. I thought of how the moon must have swung down over the stable doors, lighting up the way. How the latch on the stall must've caught and then slid open with the slightest pinch of metal against wood. But I didn't go any further than that. I'd been far enough myself.

In *Word Power Made Easy*, there was this word with several meanings. We all hated this book, but Mrs. Newell made sure it was on everyone's desk in her afternoon classes. "Mark it up, commit to it. Your SATs will be all the better for it." She enunciated each it so that the t's flew over our heads and out the windows. Outside, the days were sunny and new, breathless. Inside, I stared at the list of words on page 212. *Obstreperous, belligerent, bound, cantankerous, unpropitious, bellicose, inimical.* I focused on the little one-syllable word, crowded in by bullies. Bound by the nylon dock line in the back of Buzz's beat-up Chevy. Bound for glory, for that closet under the stairs, for a rocky beach where scraped knees were traded for kisses. Bound to end up with more homework and detentions and trouble than I'd ever be worth. Without any limits we might leap through the open windows into all that boundless blue. I considered my options, all of them out of bounds and stupid, and then realized birthday boy was leaning in through the doorway, his hands on the doorframe. Behind me, Geoffrey breathed down my neck, asking for the answers to numbers 7 and 9.

On the lake directions were like sins, cardinal and complicated. The wind came at me, warm, south by southwest, up from the oil rigs out in the Gulf. If I ever sailed there, would a roughneck dive from his platform and swim parallel to my boat? Some boys liked land better than sea. Would the one who leaned in through the doorway finally loop his arm in mine? I'd only discover his feet on solid ground, landlocked, guided by the edges of a court, call it tennis or basketball. Games geared to gardens and gymnasiums. There were clear boundaries on land. Out on the water, they weren't so clear. Joni's words cluttered my mind—*sea* and *sail* and *song* and *sinking*. Though I thought I'd known, I'd lost sense of all I wanted. I'd lost all sense of direction.

At the drive-in *BUtterfield 8* was showing. The coming attractions lit up the night and Buzz spilled a good portion of his Jack Daniels when he pushed me into the back seat. By the time Elizabeth Taylor had written *No Sale* in red lipstick across the bedroom mirror, I had rope burns around my wrists and ankles. I thought about how it all started with lipstick, and how it kept on going that way. Above me, Buzz had his eyes closed, his breath tight and insistent. The Chevy's ceiling was torn, as ragged as the feeling inside me, as rough as the nylon wringing my hands. I thought of boating knots. Rolling, clove, Lighterman's hitches. A round turn and two half hitches. A bowline. But Buzz only knew about the bitter end of the rope, the one he held in his teeth. I stared up at the screen and listened to Liz, her voice sweet and melodic, how she sounded lonely even though she pretended she wasn't.

Leon long ago gave up writing letters. I never answered, and his last note was short, never questioning, simply giving in to give up and maybe even forgive. I doubted that last bit but went ahead and gave myself permission to keep on not responding. To keep on looking past corners into the odd light of winter and then spring, green and airy, and then summer, vast and muffled and loaded with free time.

Geoffrey had taken up with a freshman girl who wore her hair in pigtails. I didn't know whether to wish her luck or pity her. And then, on the last day of school, I broke my right arm.

"Fractured, honey," my mom reminded me.

Birthday boy had waved to me from his too-small bicycle and pedaled into the dusty, maze-like traffic, and I'd waved back and thought about him the whole ride home. At my stop I stepped off the streetcar and tripped. The driver who hummed the blues acknowledged me. First time ever. Face down on St. Charles Avenue, I heard, "You all right, baby?" I sat up in the middle of the paved road and tried to gather my scattered books, the junk that fell from my open satchel, and realized I couldn't. I thought of halyards gone astray, bouncing off the mast, instead of pinioned tight. That was my arm.

Or whatever held it together.

"Well, honey, that's just your second mishap in life." My mother was clueless. She remembered my green-stick fracture, how at the age just shy of a year I'd been reluctant to nap and jumped out of my crib. She had no idea then and she'd no idea now that her daughter was bored beyond dreaming.

Until the doctor asked about the marks around my wrists.

Due North

Why is there is no such thing as north by south or east by west? Why does direction turn only slightly, instead of leaning full tilt into another place, another time, another anything? I wished for an island to occupy. Only the North Star, or a magnetic pole, to show me where I'd landed. Without doctors or mothers or boys.

I ended up on a peninsula with great aunts. I supposed that was good enough. The ship was still there, hulking, its heaving sides a battled hint of gray. I walked down to Castine's town dock and studied the slackness in the cabin cruisers' hitch lines, how they looped through rusted cleats, and the tension in the bowlines that might fall around a girl's ankle just so. My arm was in a sling and a tall midshipman, *Stanley* stenciled onto the back of his blue work shirt, stopped to admire my cast. His smile was too much, and like an idiot, I smiled back.

There was no more poetry to Lowell's hill, to the house that slowly fell down its slope, to the kisses that happened one summer ago. And there was nothing as pink and transparent as skinny little shrimp to catch in these waters, their currents too cold and secure for such fragile fish, shell or no shell. And in the boats heading out to sea, there were no promises. I wasn't allowed out on the water anyway.

I looked back at the tall midshipman and his smile. "You play Hearts?" I asked.

"Sure," he said.

And we walked down Water Street, just above the rock-covered shoreline, a half moon rising into the early evening, its direction set and sure.

WE ARE HERE BECAUSE OF A HORSE

Tulsa by night shines like a shattered gold watch.

We arrive in the pitch of early morning, that time after midnight when the world is sheathed and unspeaking. We start out late in the day and head straight into the sun, traveling black and gray roads at double the speed of racing horses. Hills and curves and rain and green, green fields of soy and corn lift themselves to us. Cherokee lands shout as we fly by. Loud and glowing, tines of pink porous light reach up to the sky in a giant sunburst, a glorified crown of gold. Somewhere in the distance are hills, or the illusion of hills, that flatten as the sun settles on the horizon. The tree line widens out and it looks as if we could drive on forever. Then the sky darkens past layers of gauzy violet into a backdrop of black cast with a thousand stars and blinking casino signs. "Angelica just won $84,138!" repeats one of the neon boards. Against the quickening night the neon is so bright that I have to look away, back to the road, to keep from driving astray, out of my lane.

Now there are smaller signs—white words on a black-green background—which advise, DO NOT DRIVE INTO SMOKE. Further on, very small road signs, most too small to read, mark the guardrail every few miles. HITCHHIKERS MAY BE ESCAPING INMATES—the words blur as we race past. I wonder about fires and prison jumpsuits, both orange and out of control. And then in the distance the city begins to glow. Here is the orange light: the signs have warned of the wrong things.

The brilliant litter of Tulsa rises from the miles and miles of dark fields where semis and SUVs scuff the quiet with a loud rushing noise. We enter the city, avoiding the Broken Arrow Expressway. Instead, we turn toward a broad avenue crowded with car lots and late-night restaurants and gas stations and urgent care centers. Hidden from this boulevard by an enclave of trees and landscaping and little roads that swoop in and out is our hotel. We follow the signs, driving in and around and down to find its massive entrance, curved and concrete. While we have missed the ancient Creek Council Oak, we have landed at its namesake, the DoubleTree Inn.

The foyer is twice the size we'd expected. The front desk receptionist's greeting is given as if it were one in the afternoon, rather than one in the morning. "Welcome! We hope you enjoy your stay." We have come to hotel-land. Somewhere, beyond the double-thick walls, there are drums. Distracted by the sound, I sign the register: Meli and Sam Henrikson. I'm handed the key cards to our room and a plate of warm oversized cookies, and we find the elevators.

"Isn't this nice?" Meli says as we travel to our floor.

Meli is my wife and only twenty-one. I am not much older at twenty-two. We are in our first months of marriage, but I've known Meli a long time. She has always astonished me. What draws her attention is very different from what slams into mine.

"Can't you hear the drums?" I ask.

Meli is eating her cookie. It doesn't even crumble.

The elevator doors glide open and we wind along a river of blue carpeting to our room. The drums seem to have stopped, or perhaps they just are muted by fourth floor walls. Our room has two double beds with double feather comforters. We have arrived in the land of double-your-money, double-timing, double-tipping, double-meaning, double-scheming moments and mementos: Tulsa-land, hotel-land, keep-our-land-grand-land.

We are here because of a horse.

The horse has disappeared from the Expo Center stall.

The horse trainer has become uncooperative. We become incomprehensive.

"What do you mean he won't go? What do you mean he won't show?" we say to the trainer. He shakes his head, looking annoyed and sad.

"Just can't," he says. "Just won't."

We are tired, but perhaps not as tired as the trainer.

Meli is quiet. She gives me that "Now what?" look.

I wonder if the horse had been a mistake. Sight unseen, Meli had taken on a yearling at a pretty price, one ready to show in the halter class. But a missing horse can't get showed. I wonder if he has been stolen. If the trainer, the man in charge, is a horse thief. If Meli's long-lost brothers might be involved. I consider calling the police. And then I begin to suspect that there never was a horse at all, that the advertisement Meli had seen in her equine news magazine had been a hoax, that we've been had.

Then I think about the story Meli has always told. Of the horse, dark and able and elegant, who stood outside her bedroom window night after night when she was a young girl. She swears it's not a dream, that it's true. She's told me many times of how she stood at the locked window with her hands on the glass, the horse's breath clouding the opposite side. How his eyes seemed black and bottomless, his mane like tattered wings, his hooves tearing at the ground so that in the morning, coming home from his night shift at the quarry, Meli's father would curse the torn earth, the spirits that dwelled on his land whenever he was away. How, once the scent of horse stayed around, her brothers and father and uncle lost their tempers elsewhere. How she found the keys to all the locks in the house and locked herself in and everyone else out.

And then one night, the night I'll always remember, Meli broke her window and climbed out and followed the horse through the yard, past her father's strangely quiet dogs, and across the fields to my family's farm. The horse remained at a distance, vigilant. "He watched over me," she told me. "And he brought me to you." Somehow Meli knew to stop at our place, the lights in the windows warm and yellow. Breathless, she gave up chasing the horse, and he moved on, a black shape against the washed-out light of dusk, the evening turning quickly to night.

And now years later, she has bought a horse, a horse promised to be dark and able and elegant, but he has disappeared, or did he never exist?

Not knowing what else to do, we decide to look for answers and head out to the "The Praying Hands" monument on the other side of town.

At the entrance to Oral Roberts University—its gold buildings, large and looming—are the hands. They are not the art deco hands-like-wings that we have pictured. They are the hands of a junkie, veined and undone. Bronzed, but not at all like military stars or baby's boots. Maybe they are the unkempt hands of a cowboy. Maybe the cowboy god will hear our prayers. But when we pray for changed luck, for a missing horse that won't go to magically appear and look up and suddenly want to go, we imagine the hands crashing down.

"Maybe we should visit the Council Tree instead," says Meli. Her eyes are moist and dark like an animal's.

"Maybe so," I say.

Unlike the other visitors, the ones posing for pictures before the statue, mimicking the bronze hands by clasping their own above their heads, Meli shrugs her shoulders and leaves her hands, unpraying and limp, at her sides.

We haven't always been this way, Meli and me. Once we were younger, kids with kid-sized dreams. Life went along, simple and easy, until we took on bulkier ideas, double-sized dreams. Like the horse.

We are just having a black-cloud moment, that's all.

The Council Tree.

Once the Creek Indians came from Alabama, driven westward for all the wrong reasons. They stopped at the edge of the Arkansas River and left the ashes of grandmothers and great-grandfathers beside the greatest oak they'd ever seen. Now there is a park, a placard, a tribute to this place.

Meli points up into the branches. Black crows nudge the bark with their blacker beaks.

"What's wrong with those birds?" Meli says.

I continue looking up. The crows crowd together, a pitch-colored mass, like a live abscess, unsettled and growing.

"There are too many," I answer.

"And they're too quiet for crows," Meli decides.

The birds seem to sleep.

Northeast of the oak, a direction the crows might have flown, the Boston Avenue Methodist Church reaches up to the sky like an arrow. Along its tower are wings of golden glass. The tower soars and flies up to heaven while anchored in place between the Broken Arrow and Cherokee Expressways. We drive into the parking lot, fringed with white poles and red banners, and sit there in the truck, looking up at the vast church. It has beauty and greatness, but this cannot help us. And so we drive on.

Meli wants a root beer, and I don't know what I want anymore.

We follow 21st Street to S. Peoria. If we kept on heading north, parallel to the Arkansas River and past the crosshairs of three elevated highways, we'd come to Cain's Ballroom. I imagine Bob Wills and Tex Ritter belting tunes above the spring-loaded, dime-a-dance floors heavy with boots and ladies' heels. I drum my hands along the steering wheel and stop when Meli glares at me.

A historical sign declares this part of town Brookside, once Creek Indian land, crossed by the Chisholm Trail and roving cattle. Now there are brick bungalows, flower shops, bakeries, bookstores, laundromats, Billy Sims BBQ, and Weber's Superior. I imagine giving up the country to live in the city, and Meli waves at the little orange building. Weber's has become the landmark we've driven past on the way to the Expo Center these past few days. The sign screams root beer. We park and order our food to go and then sit on the truck's tailgate to eat.

I have two double cheeseburgers and a paper tray of tater tots. Meli is sipping her root beer and munching down onion rings. I've always wondered how she can be so delicate with her drink and manhandle her food all at once.

An old Buick moves past, and black smoke pours from its tailpipe and Jeff Tweedy's voice from its radio. I glance at Meli. Lyrics tumble towards us, all out of order: *double kick summer, river love, she fell, and she fell. Another drum, another drummer.* Something tribal is happening. All these drums. Meli is staring past me, mouthing the words, placing them back in order, but she doesn't smile.

"There was no point in our coming here," she says.

Her face reveals no expression, a flatline look that refuses to tell all. But this reaction is something I've gotten used to. Underneath it all I know is a pulse that once quickened will not slow. Like a tempest it will find a way out, wordless but telling all too much.

"There was a point," I say. "We just have to hope for the best."

"I'm done hoping." Meli tosses a crumb to a gathering of sparrows. They dot the asphalt parking lot, gray on gray. A small, scrappy one wins the largest piece of trash.

"You have to be like that one." I point to the bird.

"What? A tough little shit?"

"Yeah," I say. "A tough little shit."

Back at the hotel, frustration flies around the room.

Meli throws a glass against the wall opposite our bed.

"What the hell?" I say.

Iced tea is all over the bed and glass shards all over the room. A lemon slice lands near the TV.

"You'll have to call for housekeeping," Meli says.

"No kidding."

I lift the receiver and call the front desk. "There's been an accident—no, not 911. Just sheets, blankets. A vacuum cleaner. Yes, thank you."

I open the door to the hallway and hear the drums again. Not sweet bopping Wilco drums. Something heavier. Meli disappears into the bathroom. I hear the lock click into place.

The last time Meli locked herself in, she was twelve. She hid from her dad in the closet. She hid from her uncle in her father's room. She hid from her brothers in the den with the shotguns. She considered her sisters lucky they'd never been born. And then she found the drawer where all the keys were hidden and locked herself into her own bedroom. Before anyone could find her, she broke the nailed-shut window, and clambered and scraped her way out.

Down the road, several pastures away, we were the neighbors who kept to ourselves. Thirteen and unsure, I didn't know there was any other way to be. Until that night, when Meli climbed through my window. She made it seem her privilege, as if hiding in the room of a boy she hardly knew was normal. Every detail that evening stood out to me, even long after. Once Meli arrived, everything changed. My days of being a loner ended. Long afternoons reading Steinbeck and Salinger, my parents' big book of American poets, were soon traded for wondering what girls were all about. Especially this girl.

The late September sky was a flat blue. The dim autumn evenings came earlier now, with a coolness that lingered. After chores, I'd kick off my boots and walk through the grass, already damp, and search for the rising moon or the first planet beyond a five-fingered reach. That night my father had taken over my chores and told me to study. Instead, I stared over my desk out the window.

The wind had died down and you could hear the cows lowing. Wildflowers trimmed the fields and the roadside with yellow and black and cream. Not swaying and tipping as they had that afternoon, but stock still: outlines of wild carrot and coneflowers and thistle. Eventually, they became silhouettes, and I could hear my mother whistling a Dale Evans tune and washing dishes. The sound of the spigot turning on and off.

And then there was a glimpse of dark hair, dungarees, a slip of something at the roadside. She moved inside the shadows and brushed through the ditch weed, her place marked only by the way the tall grasses waved and quieted. I'd seen her before, but not off on her own.

Most times it was from the bus in the afternoon, when we'd round the bend and the boys around me called mean things out the windows, me quiet and staring through the dusty glass. Meli sat on her father's porch, its railings crowded on one side by skinny trees that gave hardly any shade, the naked yard home to three dogs, tied up and seldom barking. She always looked dirty, like she didn't have a mother to comb her hair. I wondered why she wasn't in school with me.

Now she squatted in my yard. The tangled green grass buried her sneakers, and she scratched the inside of an ankle. "Because we'll meet again," my mother sang from the kitchen, and the day became night, a bruised sky turning the roadside flowers black and the girl blue.

"Indigo," she said later. "Not blue, an old indigo."

"Faded," I had to agree.

But that was after she came up to the window, after her face slammed into the sill as she pushed herself into the room. My pencils and pens spilled from their mason jar and fell to the floor. She climbed over my desk and stepped on my open math book, kicking a ruler and sending a compass spinning. I sat sideways in my chair, not moving, and stared at her eyes, only inches from my own. They were dark brown, with streaks of violet at the edges. A color I'd only seen in twilight. Never in anyone's gaze.

She was slight and thin and breathed short stiff breaths. I thought of horses, the way they exhale in heavy sighs after a good lope. Her hair was long and knotted with straw and twigs, but what I noticed most of all were the cuts and bruises. Across one cheek, a jagged, mean-looking mark where the blood had already begun to cake, and more nicks and scratches on her knuckles and arms. She looked like a stray who'd only recently become stray, soiled and wild and lost, but not smelly.

"I'm Sam," I said.

"I know," she answered. "I hear your mother call you sometimes."

"This is my room," I said. I tried to look the boss, the owner of my room.

"It's nice," she said.

"Why are you in it?"

"I was looking for my horse." She looked around.

"You don't have a horse, and even if you did, he's not in here."

"I'm Meli." She looked down at her feet now. Her sneakers were gray and had no laces.

"All right," I said. "But my mom will probably just take you back home."

"I don't live there anymore." Her voice seemed to crack. "I live here now. With you."

"Some times are happy, and some are just blue," my mother sang, starting the song again. Her voice floated into the darkening night.

"My dad will definitely take you back home."

But Meli stayed.

And now, years later, she was in our hotel bathroom, and I was wishing we'd never come for that horse.

Housekeeping knocks.

I open the door and two women enter. They wear green pantsuit uniforms. One has black hair in shoulder-length waves around her long face. The other has copper hair, kinked and very long, some of it piled on top of her head like a crown. Right away, I think of them as black-haired girl and copper-haired girl.

Still, somewhere down the hall, those drums again—a dull repetitive thumpa-thump. It may be an exhaust fan; it may be my mind.

The girls seem not to notice the sound. They have nothing with them. They have come to assess the situation.

Black-haired girl says, "I told you we'd need a full set of bedding."

Copper-haired girl only nods.

They gather up the damp covers and quilts and walk past me out the door.

I sit on the end of the bed and wonder if they'll come back. We may be sleeping in tea-soaked sheets. That doesn't bother me. It's the shards of glass that bother me.

The night Meli came to my house, my mother eventually came in and found us. At first she seemed startled, but then took Meli and cleaned her up—the cuts, the bruises, her clothes. My father—the lawyer, the landowner, a man known for being fair—phoned the authorities. Family services.

Meli's father was found dead, the brothers arrested, then imprisoned. The uncle gone. Meli's mother, long gone.

And so Meli stayed with us.

Black-haired girl and copper-haired girl whisk about the room.

I try to stay out of their way. The bedding is nearly changed, and the glass hurls around inside the Hoover. I know that Meli has only thrown the glass out of frustration; she has thrown things before.

Black-haired girl turns to me, and I see her mouth move. I hear only the roar of the vacuum. I imagine black crows flying out of her black hair. Still, she persists, leaning closer. Something about the comforter—that it's missing.

Copper-haired girl switches off the vacuum, and the room is too quiet too quickly.

"Are you crazy?" she says.

Black-haired girl looks at me—and I wonder if I am crazy—and back at her copper-haired girl. "What do you mean, crazy?"

"You took the comforter downstairs," says copper-haired girl to black-haired girl. "You took it down with everything else."

"Unh," black-haired girl says and pushes through the door and drags herself back down the hall.

I remember one afternoon when Meli stood outside my room. Fifteen and no longer in dungarees. Her legs were as long as a filly's, and a floral skirt brushed her knees. She hummed a song I didn't know and stared past me.

When Meli had first come to live with us, my mother changed the sewing room into a bedroom. Together, they'd moved the old Singer to a corner and painted the little room a pale lavender. Meli learned to use the sewing machine and made pillow covers to match the bedspread. The room glowed with colors the house had never seen: all variations of blue. Meli guided layers of fabric through the machine, and in the evenings we would hear it whirring and Meli humming along, her voice curving and threading while the material fell to the floor in bright mounds.

On that afternoon, though, she got home from school and lingered in the kitchen, bumping into things on purpose, then came to my room but stayed just outside.

"What's wrong?" I asked.

She nodded at the window, then looked at me.

"That was the way in," she said. She seemed to consider what she'd say next, as if speaking would ruin something. For a moment she shouldered the doorjamb and then pushed off, finally entering my room, a space she'd never been shy of before.

"Yeah, it was," I said.

"So which way is out?"

"It depends," I said, playing along, following her even though she tended to wander into rough territory. She seemed to head in directions she knew well, which frightened me, though made me curious. Journeys that began in her head and ended up realities, adventures. Wayward and resolute in her invitations, she'd pull me along and I always accepted. Ever since I'd seen her on her own porch, years ago, there was something about her that went right through me. The way she sat with her chin in her hands, looking off into the distance, the three dogs lying in the dust of the yard. But now she was here in my room, and she might just turn and walk away. I knew then I would always be right there. Beside her. And so I answered, "It all depends on where you're going, what you're looking for."

Black-haired girl arrives with a thick bundle.

She opens an enormous plastic bag and pulls out the new comforter. Quickly the room is filled with feathers and down. Gray and white bits of fluff. I recall the swarm of sparrows in the parking lot at lunch. Meli is still in the bathroom, missing the show.

I run to close our suitcases.

"What the—?" says black-haired girl.

Copper-haired girl has just finished coiling up the vacuum cleaner's cord. She holds out her hands and bats at the feathers. She clasps her hands together as if in prayer to the god of housekeeping. And then she laughs. She laughs and laughs and laughs. I laugh too. It is funny. The room is full of feathers. It looks as though a fox has been in the room. It looks as though it's snowing in September. It looks as though black-haired girl is unhappy.

She looks at copper-haired girl: it is an impatient, I-told-you-so look. A look that makes no sense. She shakes the comforter. More feathers fly out. The comforter's hem is open; I wonder if it had ever been sewed closed. Unfinished like one of Meli's larger projects that involved several layers of work—pinning and tucking and hand-stitching followed by the thrumming mechanics of the sewing machine. Or perhaps the hem is torn, a seam-ripper's work. Somewhere a seamstress is frowning. And then I think again of Meli. At this kind of missing step, she herself would be smiling and laughing her head off.

Black-haired girl glares at copper-haired girl. "Now you're gonna have to vacuum all over again," she says.

But her coworker is too busy laughing to take offense.

Black-haired girl drags the torn comforter out of the room and down the hallway and copper-haired girl follows her, laughing and laughing.

And still those drums, incessant—a blunt, monotonous background to our afternoon. I peer around the doorway. All the way down the hall feathers are flying, drifting the corridor like dirty snow, like giant dust motes. Copper-haired girl is howling now, and black-haired girl punches her arm, though she is smiling back at me when she does this. A few doors open and puzzled guests look out at the uniformed girls and the sifting, sinking down and dander. A man across the hall looks after the girls and then at me. His gaze is accusatory.

I cannot help myself and ask him very loudly, "Do you hear the drums?"

He slams his door. Behind me the bathroom door opens and Meli peeks out. She sees the drifting down, frowns, and comes out to stand with me in the doorway. She kisses me hard on the mouth. I kiss her back.

When I was seventeen and Meli was sixteen, she leaned up and kissed me for the first time. I was working on my father's truck, bent over the engine, hands covered with grease, and she tapped me on the shoulder. I held the spark plug I'd just removed and turned around. Nearly as tall as me, she reached around my neck and pulled my face to hers. Startled, I felt how warm her palms were and saw how her mouth opened slightly. She seemed to know what she was doing, and so I closed my eyes and tried to follow along. At first I had my arms out so as not to smudge her sundress, but then let the spark plug drop into the dirt. I touched her narrow waist and the folds of cloth that fell across her hips and then found her bare back. With each movement, my hands blackened the material and eventually her skin.

It was just a kiss. But it was Meli who was doing the kissing. I was gone. That was it. As clichéd as it sounds, I was carried off to a place unreal and confounding, one I never wished to lose hold of. I stopped thinking for the first time ever and let a tangle of sensations slam around inside me—breaths, scents, murmurs—all sweet and daunting. Even in the act of kissing, Meli seemed caught up in her own world, one that I just happened to belong to. Later, there would be times I felt diminished, as if all her brightness made me the shadow.

Sometimes she'd wake me in the middle of the night and pull me outside, to see the stars, to lie down in the middle of an empty field and remind me just how small we were. The wind might brush over us, Meli barelegged and wrapping herself around me for warmth. We'd rest there, limbs entwined, and stare at the sky. At dawn we'd arrive back home, running, tired but newly awake, damp but not cold.

My mother wasn't sure of this twist in our friendship, how it seemed to float out of nowhere, a ribboned, uncertain thing. A few months went by and our disappearances didn't go unnoticed. She took Meli aside and had a talk with her. And she had my father take me aside. He grumbled about it but took me outside to the fence line anyway.

We stood with our soles on the lowest rail and pretended to survey the livestock, in particular the lone pig. He would never make pork because my father had become fond of him.

"What's going on here?" he asked me.

"Sir?" I said.

"Don't hedge, Sam." He handled his pipe but didn't light it. "You getting serious or what?" My father, a man who had feelings but didn't like to talk of them, was asking me about love.

"I guess so," I said.

"Well, that's indefinite. Don't you know a good thing when it's right in front of you?" He paused and then said under his breath, "Sometimes you youngsters have no idea."

"Sir?"

"No idea!" he said, almost shouting. "Think about this thing you're doing." And here he looked at me, slightly squinting. "And be careful." Then he walked back to the house and left me standing there.

The pig was rooting around in the mud. I reached around in the mess of my mind, uncertain of what my father had just advised, and found only muck and hesitation. I wasn't sure what would happen. I was merely going along, and something new was happening. Something that I didn't want to define or understand; something I just wanted to be in the middle of.

The drumbeat is growing louder.

Meli gives me a look and then she glances down the hallway, and I know she finally hears the drums. I take her hand, and we follow the sound. Doors repeat themselves all the way down to the end of the corridor. Their numbers are all even: 418, 420, 422. I wish for one of these doors to slam open, to know the beat is simply Tweedy and his boys bouncing through an album session, that the loft in Chicago didn't work out and so now they are here in hotel-land. I wish for the walls to come down, for an answer on the other side.

Meli pulls me along. At the end of the hall is a window and another door—the emergency exit. A stairwell. The drums vibrate more loudly as I push open the door and we walk down the stairs.

Four flights down is a large room, a solarium of sorts. A pool glows under the day's softening sun. Here the tremor of the drumbeat can be seen on the water's surface. A constant rippling. The beat seems to sound from under the pool. Meli holds my hand more tightly but seems mesmerized and draws me closer to the pool's edge. I am confused and stop looking for the source of the drums. I look only at the pool, at the shallowest and then the deepest ends. There are cerulean tiles around the edges and at the bottom a large design. It is deep blue, almost black. Barelegged, Meli begins to ease an ankle into the shuddering pool. Her hand slips out of mine, and I feel off balance. She is gone, swimming down to the darkest, deepest part of the pool.

"Meli?" I call.

I cannot see her and panic. Below, at the pool's depths, an underwater image wavers and rears up, horse-like. Mane flowing, hooves blinding, nostrils wide, sides heaving.

And then I dive and the water is all around me. I hold my breath and open my eyes to the watery light. Meli is bathed in this light, strangely alive in this light. She swims away from me and climbs the steps at the shallow end, her heels lifting and then disappearing. I come to the surface and tread water, staring at my wife, a blurred wet picture that I can't make any sense of.

Meli has always been the half of me that breathes when I am unsure of how to take a breath. Even after our wedding, after the gold bands had slipped onto our fingers, I couldn't grasp the meaning of what we'd done. I felt as though I was still following, even though I'd been the one to propose and set things in motion—that summer before graduate school and the teaching fellowship, a house with a studio for Meli's design work, a community garden where we worked with friends and family.

It was all there, a little too perfect when viewed from the outside. But I was inside. And Meli was there, perfectly imperfect, with her days of silence broken by the sound of shattering glass, by the brilliant fragments that lit up the house. Glass-fronted cabinets littered the kitchen counters, a collection of jelly glasses hit the pantry walls, stemmed glasses kept only their stems. I noted the quiet that always followed.

Meli would act as if nothing had happened, and then it would start up again. Slowly, with a promise of continuing calm until that taut stare took over. She puzzled me with her round ways of seeing the world. The purpose with which she drew up dress patterns. The way she'd work in the garden, speak to my mother by phone, arrange flowers, prepare meals. And then her mood would tighten and her dark almond eyes would gaze unblinking into the mornings, the afternoons.

One of those afternoons Meli asked me to drive her to Tulsa.

"It's the horse," she'd said. "He's there."

And so we went. No matter the work I had to do, I loaded the truck and we went.

The horse has become the black shadow that lengthens between us.

Meli sits in her newly made bed and stares straight ahead. Her hair is still wet and scattered in thick strands around her shoulders. Outside our window is a blanket of blue sky tipped with the dark green tops of pine and spruce. Three miles away is the Expo Center where a stall remains mysteriously empty. The trainer lies and says that he's put out a search for the horse; I wonder how anyone can find a horse that's never existed. We've been fooled, and it's time to go home.

Meli turns her head to me and I begin telling her things.

"I imagine when your horse was younger, he was spindly-legged and covered with dirt, kept out in a corral by himself. From a distance he probably looked more like a big black dog than a horse. Once you might have stood on the bottom rail of the fence and looked out at him. But surely he didn't come to you."

"He would have been a beauty," Meli says and her eyes fill with dark tears. "He would have." Now she looks at me, nearly through me. "You just don't understand what happened. You never have."

"What?"

"You don't have to understand." Her voice tilts toward anger.

"But I want to," I say.

"You don't have to, though."

Her words are like a wall, but I know I will wait. I'll wait until she breaks the words like she's broken so many glasses. I'll wait until she is finally able to tell me. Until she is brave enough to come out of the room where she once hid, where she eyed the stallion at the window, where she still hid, even now. That Meli has lived in the past for too long, that we made this trip—the whole damned thing is an enormous, stumbling mistake. I will wait. Even if it takes until that horse is old and grizzled. Even if it takes forever.

We drive down Tulsa's roads.

It is late afternoon, already October, and the world is turning orange. We have been here for five days. Autumn is chasing us down, wrapping up the trees in mirrored light. The evenings are getting colder. It's long since time to go.

We pass the gold university buildings, the "Praying Hands" that seem to pry open the heavens, the thick-trunked Council Oak with branches that scrape the ground, and along the Arkansas River where skeletal oil rigs slant sideways and cast shadows. The Broken Arrow Expressway leads us out of town, southeast, tipping down and down, back to where we started. Highway 51: it is our own Trail of Tears.

We make our way past casinos and sheep farms, gas stations and the bottle green of broken glass, broken hearts, cornfields. Here, there is no smoke to drive into. There are no hitchhikers. The road narrows and we enter a small town, its thoroughfare lined with creameries, convenience stores, and churches. The houses here are pretty, old, charming even. And then the road opens to more fields that roll themselves out like swathes of jade cloth.

"Look," Meli says, pointing out the truck window.

In the distance a horse stands alone, its dark head angled into the breeze, a double-barreled silhouette that burns a hole straight into the sky.

SKYLIGHT

What's round on the ends and high in the middle? Chloe remembers
only this. Her first inkling that Ohio even existed. To her, the smell of sugar
and sweat, the days bathed in humidity, backlit with pink and yellow light,
and measured by how long James Booker held that one eye closed, or that
note on a beat-up piano—nearly forever—these were the familiar things.
Louisiana knew nothing of Ohio. Surely Ohio knew nothing of Louisiana.
But now, years later, she looks into the gray-blue sky, scarred by jet trails and
the burden of clouds, and it is the sky of Columbus, not New Orleans. She
traces the trails south, as if they could send her back home.

Simon draws his hand across her collarbone, finding her naked shoulders.
More trails. She feels his breath against the side of her neck as he asks how
long she's been here. She doesn't turn to respond, the sheets tucked under
her arms, and stares straight ahead. There is a skylight above her bed, the bed
she invited him into last night. Only now she can't think of why. He asks too
many questions, like this one, which she would rather not answer.

    "Come on," he says. "Seriously, how can a person live in a city for nine-
teen years and not call it home?"

    Like the clouds—unmoving white nimbus, filled with promises and
air—he rests there against her, persistent, heavy, uninteresting. She wishes
for *pain perdu*, the lost bread of lost lives, simple, sweet, dusted in sugar and
berries.

* * *

The night before, at the Rumba Café, the crowd streamed back and forth between the bar and the patio and the seats before the small stage. Megan Palmer and the Hopefuls played their second set, and between orders Chloe caught the glint of the bass guitar, Megan's bow sliding across the strings of her fiddle, a scattering of dancers mostly bouncing to the music. The dark wood of the bar and the pressed iron ceiling, the color of old crawfish shells, made the brightest evening feel like night, and Chloe knew she craved the darkness since she couldn't have the light off the bayou, the clouds billowing with rose gold.

Bartending came easily, so different from her days at Ohio State, and Chloe leaned into the ease of the job, the same job she'd had back home, the Rumba not so different from the Maple Leaf. Like the stretching, lingering notes across the room, Chloe stretched again for the tap, filling another glass with Stella, and hoped she'd know what to do next. The man sitting by himself at the bar stared at her, and she knew that by the end of the night he'd still be there, good-looking and certain and convinced that she'd have him. And because his name was Simon, so simple, so seemingly uncomplicated, and because Megan sang the song that began, "love wishes for confusion," she knew she'd let him.

In a series of evenings at the Wexner Theater, Charlie Chaplin swings his cane, smiling at the street girl; Richard Bausch reads from one of his stories, and the main character, a woman, leans over a stroller, admiring the baby and weeping; Gus Van Sant escapes up the stairs as his film, *Mala Noche*, begins.

"You know you love it here," Simon says. "Just look at all this."

All what? Chloe thinks. She has known all this before. At a party on Audubon Place at the age of seventeen, she meets the Panovs; at a college reading at Newcomb, she witnesses Lillian Hellman throw her lit cigarette into a trash can and smoke begin to rise; the Loyola professor she sleeps with in her early twenties screens 16 mm reels of *Modern Times* and *City Lights*, the projector's light streaming over the thin covers of his bed.

"Seriously," Simon says.

She wishes to be twenty again, to lie in a bed without the white light of the sky pouring over her, to feel the professor's hands, to feel things for the first time.

Her apartment lies directly under the Columbus Metropolitan Airport's flight path. Boeing 737's, DC-9's, and MD-80's rattle her walls. She lies on her back while Simon attempts a batch of lost bread. French toast, he calls it. He is from the heartland and doesn't understand his mistake, that the French would never call this toast, the importance of words and meanings as lost to him as the sad rusks of baguette he dips in a bowl of beaten eggs and cream and nutmeg. He has burned the first three pieces. Above Chloe, the skylight window. Above the window, the clouds are lifting. Beyond the clouds, small, winged airplanes.

"They look like toys," she says.

But really, she thinks, they look like damselflies, tiny, insubstantial, coming and going. Mostly going. With transparent wings, the bayou at their backs, they whir past, moving in straight lines. Six-year-old Chloe follows them with her gaze, her hand moving, pointing. Her mother catches Chloe's chin between her fingers and squeezes. "Eat your lunch," she says, leaning over the picnic table. "You can play after." There is egg salad made with homemade mayonnaise and sweet pickles. Even under the longleaf pines, it is too hot to eat.

She teaches a film class at Ohio State.

"The Ohio State University," Simon says, pointing at the letterhead of the class syllabus.

American directors. Van Sant, Cassavetes, Anders, Jarmusch, Bog-danovich, Sayles, Bigelow, Nichols, Kubrick, Lynch, and Coppola. Her students beg for them, then complain about the number of viewings, how much work there is.

"Which Coppola?" Simon asks.

Chloe is becoming tired of his questions.

"Sofia," she says.

He responds, "That's my girl," then blinks, his eyes filled with morning light, and something else. Secrets? He swallows after he speaks.

Chloe wonders who is Simon's girl, Sofia or her.

Simon has charred half a baguette.

"How do you get this stuff to brown without burning?" He isn't mad, only asking.

Chloe wants to say, It's not that hard. Instead, she says nothing and opens the door.

Her dress is waistless and falls just above her knees, like the ones her mother dressed her in for school. And like the mornings before school at her mother's breakfast table, she has no intention of eating much. Pistachia Vera, the bakery with the best *pain au chocolat* in German Village, also has skylights. Chloe will watch squares of sun land on her croissant; she will wish for the strawberries her grandmother brought every spring Sunday. "Wait," her mother would say. "Wait until everyone is sitting and we've said grace."

Pistachia Vera is green with mid-morning light. Simon leans over the glass case, and the girl behind the counter suggests Parisian *macarons*, made of meringue, soft and weightless as air, every flavor, every hue imaginable. Black raspberry hibiscus, lavender orange honey, lemon ginger and matcha. Chloe finds the assortment pretty, but pointless. Until she tastes one and it disappears over her tongue like no kiss she's ever known. She imagines a damselfly's wings might taste as ephemeral, sheer strands of sweetness, gone as soon as they land, as soon as they've left you with the sense that you've remembered something you'd forgotten. Round on the outside and high in the middle. Something that makes you want to cry.

Here in Columbus, there is the Cup O Joe Sweetheart Mocha instead of coffee thick with chicory. Here in Columbus, there are girls that chew gum when they speak to you, the pink mass swelling between their teeth, as they pause and say, "Like, you know?" Here in Columbus, students cross College Avenue outside the crosswalks and campus buses slow and let them reach the other side. Here, behind the clouds that rise out of the river valley, is the Ohio that is round and high.

Chloe gazes up over her book at a man who is crossing inside the lines of the crosswalk. Even from a distance, this man, this director, this Gus Van Sant seems kind, and she tries to think of him before *Cowboy* and *Cowgirls* and *Elephant* and *Milk*. She thinks of *Paris, Je T'aime*, a film she's never shown her students, but one that she watches alone when Simon has gone home and the patch of window above her bed is black without stars or moon or anything. She imagines Gus in her bed, brown-eyed and brotherly, taking a break from his boyfriends, eating from the tin of popcorn her grandmother has sent all the way from Lake Catherine. It is layered with caramel and almonds, and Gus takes handfuls, but eats slowly.

"Maybe we knew each other in another time, another era," Simon says. "There's really something special about your look."

Chloe nearly chokes, but the wine she is drinking is dark red and would stain, so she doesn't. Simon needs to stop. He is quoting lines from "Le Marais," the Van Sant moment of the film Chloe doesn't share. She glares at him and thinks, There is nothing special about my look. Blond and small, she disappears inside afternoons, more cigarette smoke than perfume, ill at ease and clawing her way up to the top of understanding.

It's been weeks since she and Simon have made love. That she does understand.

She is eight years old and a light blue ribbon is falling out of her hair. She wishes for her grandmother's smile, her mother's fingers fastened around her chin, the bless-us-oh-Fathers around the Sunday table, laid with lace and potato salad and enormous Gulf shrimp still confined inside their thick, glistening skins. Oyster shells line the driveway, and when the aunts and uncles pull up in their trucks, the shells scatter and sigh under the tires. Twelve years later, Chloe thinks about soul mates. The Loyola professor leans toward her, but she knows he's not the one. He quotes silent films, his lips moving soundlessly. The nearly twenty years spent upriver cannot save her. She's naked and falling through the night sky, straight through the skylight and into her own bed.

"Maybe you should get a dog," Simon says.

Chloe breathes into the phone's receiver. She coils a strand of hair around her finger. "A nervous habit young girls should be careful about," her mother says, looking past the schoolbooks on the kitchen table to the open window. Outside, a lilac tree is in bloom. The scent is overpowering.

"Your hair is like light," the professor says, his hand reaching under the table, a waiter pausing near them and then moving on.

"Like buttercream," Simon says, taking a bite of his *macaron*. The girls behind the counter at Pistachia Vera all stare at him because he's worth it. Chloe knows she may be his blond buttercream, his southern thing, sweet between the sheets, but he's just on loan.

"Something small that doesn't bark too much." Simon is still a fool and will soon be packing for California where he belongs.

Chloe holds the phone away from her ear and is not sorry when the cross-town connection drops.

Chloe wakes up one morning. She is still in Columbus. Or is this all just a dream? Gus is frying up the *pain perdu*. He winks and pours the coffee. He knows how easy it is to live in Columbus. Maybe not so exciting, but easy. He prefers Paris, New Orleans, San Francisco. But for the moment he's here, and he knows a place that roasts its coffee with chicory. A large brown bag of Louisiana coffee along with a used espresso maker sits on the kitchen counter, and Gus fusses over steamed milk. Chloe's latte is layered with a design that reminds her of the ferns in her grandmother's back garden. Chloe stands near a cluster of green, nodding heads and her grandmother says, "I don't grow them, but they come. Birds eat the seeds, and well, you know, the ferns, they show up."

Simon is gone for good. Chloe knows she doesn't belong to him, that the months they spent together were more hollow than filled, that they aren't soul mates. "It's time," he says, weeks earlier. "Time to fly."

She imagines him as an MD-80, cutting a trail across the sky over Columbus and disappearing into the west. After he leaves, she feels as though she is disappearing too. That's when Gus shows up. He knows how to take care of a girl so that she'll stop disappearing, like smoke, like perfume. Though Gus is a figment of her less-than-dressed mind, Chloe appreciates this. She looks to him for morning coffee, for assurance.

They wind over the Old Delaware Road east-northeast of Columbus, the gray byway ribboning under a broad, blue sky. It is June and the fields are lush with calf-high corn, wheat thick and waving, low spreading stripes of soybeans. There are no Cypress trees standing in flats of brackish bayou water, but llamas mass together under a lone expanse of oaks. Gus points out that they are Swamp Whites, the oaks, and Andean, the llamas. Gus has bought a Ford F-100, which is nearly as old as he is. It is bottle green and Chloe imagines he will use it in his next film. But he says he bought it to take them places. From point A to point B and beyond.

The green truck turns up Blue Road, where there is a small farmhouse for sale. Chloe smiles at Gus and shakes her head no. Gravel sings under the tires as Gus puts the truck in reverse, and Chloe longs for the blinding white oyster shell drive of Lake Catherine. She senses that she will wake up soon, that Gus and his truck will disappear, and she will be alone again with only nights at the Rumba and days at the university to keep her company.

Schiller Park. The day is a muted blue. Gus is walking the dog, a pug named Lily, across a grassy expanse. The little dog pulls at the leash, and Gus shouldn't, but he lets her. She wants to reach the cluster of ferns as quickly as possible. Her place. Chloe sits on a bench and closes her eyes. She thinks of James Booker, that one eye forever closed, light and music pouring from his fingers.

"Do you believe in soul mates?" she hears. She thinks it's her imagination, but it's a man with a Super-8 camera and he's filming Gus and Lily.

"Sit still and smile," says her mother. But her grandmother comes into the living room and rattles the walls with her voice. "That's a moving picture camera. That child doesn't have to sit still. Better she runs than sits still."

Chloe stands up and, with the grass of Schiller Park all around her, runs toward the lens of the Super-8.

"There she goes," says the professor. "I always knew she'd go far."

She is laughing and running and hears Gus calling and Lily barking.

"Butter and light and the right temperature." Simon holds up the pan, showing off his golden points of lost bread. "That's all that's needed."

Chloe runs past the camera, her arms spread open, and the lens zeros in on her and how she moves farther and farther away, a line of light and gossamer, tracking straight through the afternoon and into the rest of her life.

THE BIKER AND THE GIRL

A **line along the road, a glint of metal**, the hum of a motor growing louder, a levee and then a river. This was the place. This was the first instance. A view from a distance which reeled itself in so close that it became unmanageable and overwhelming. He had a reason to be there, though. A job. Construction, but still it was something. It was the late '70s, and something in those days was a lot better than nothing.

He rode a trim black Harley. From his perspective, wind was everything. The bike took him places; sometimes he was surprised at where he ended up. Once at a bar where oysters and local bottled beer were pitched generously across the counter; once at a café where sunflower sprouts were loaded like afterthoughts onto plates of yellow omelettes served by girls as trim as his bike. One of the girls lingered in his mind the way she never lingered at the tables she served. Her movement was long and easy, her open smile not meant to flatter or please, until one evening as she collected silverware from his table, he put his hand over hers.

In that moment she thought she knew him from before, but she didn't know him at all. He surprised her, and she liked that. A lot. A little too much. His gaze, like reflective river water, revealed his interest in her. And the way he sat forward, his upper body taut and strong, made her pause. She found him intriguing, marked with a dark roughness. A roughness and a lean, bearded, gentle kind of danger—so that she bent forward, fork and butter knife in her grasp, the heat of his hand over hers, and said, "What?"

"I want to take you somewhere," he said.

"All right," she said, unfazed, even reassured by his straightforward desire. "I get off in an hour. You can come back then." She leaned in and whispered, "Okay?"

Her breath was warm and fragrant on his cheek. His eyes narrowed. He was calmed and riled all at once. That her answer was so clear, exactly what he wanted to hear, amazed him; somehow he felt mocked. As if she might just play along for fun, not for fun. He expected as much and nodded.

"I'll be back at seven." He pushed his seat out and stood, watching her turn and walk back to the kitchen.

A crow covered with parasites, one wing torn so that its pinfeathers cocked out, watched from an oak tree. From its branch high above the levee, it could see the river and the river road, both stretching and bending for miles. The breeze was good at this height, strong and unerring. Barges bright with rust, pushed along by tugboats, drew lines in the river, leaving gray-white wakes behind them. Trash floated along the shoreline—tires, bottles, a lawn chair with its green-and-white webbing still attached.

The crow eyed something shiny down the road. As it moved along, it caught the March sun, the passing clouds, glinting and darkening. The crow danced for a small moment up and down the branch, and then as the motorcycle roared past, stretched its wings and flew off.

Against the sky the crow appeared a black smudge, a smirch of doubt, an unlikely thing. The biker squinted, looking up, then forward at the next sharp bend in the road. As he took the curve, a shadow fell away from his bike, long like the afternoon. A perfect outline. Somewhere his three-year-old daughter might have been standing in the same sun, looking at her own shadow. The road narrowed.

He imagined his daughter, like her mother, asking for yet another story. Another story about the places she'd never seen, her hair tangled and her cheeks hot and tear-stained. Only, his daughter would eventually be satisfied, and then she'd stand on the sidewalk outside their house and draw with a nub of colored chalk, the sun all around her.

The biker pulled into the lot next to his apartment building, a brown one-story with a flat roof and low ceilings. He gripped the brake, crushing and settling gravel under his wheels. The '76 Harley had already seen some miles in the past two years, mostly in California along the coast. Warehouse jobs, beaches, other girls. The biker never stayed in one place very long. Not since the one girl had latched on, had told him she was pregnant. Instead, he found himself attached to new places. To a way of life that didn't demand anything.

He craved motion, the lonely roll of the road and the sharp keen of the wind, echoing even after he'd stopped for a while. Straight shots, mountain passes, the vivid green of pastures. The pale, denuded pink of the desert. A blur of asphalt, white lines, a deer left rotting at the shoulder. He smelled each town as he entered it—brackish water of the bayou in Plaquemines Parish; the sharp odor of a sugar refinery along the river outside Arabi; sulfur from a plant in Ascension, its tall stacks sending out plumes, thick and orange. Louisiana felt truer, heavier, something he could understand.

At times his neighbors sat out in the evening, talking and drinking beer. The aroma of shrimp and crawfish, newspaper spread over a folding table to catch the pink, the red, the luminous shells, and the hard crusted heads of the shellfish as their soft bodies disappeared by the mouthful. There was a way the days fell into each other, one after the other, warm and unencumbered. He didn't even mind the work; he'd had worse. Somehow he had become a part of this place. His rides were now limited and local. There was no fear of returning to the places he'd been, no fear of reliving the damage he'd done. It was still out there; there was nothing to correct. Slowly he'd settled, become a permanent fixture, acquiring things—belongings that allowed him to belong. The road was no longer wide; he still headed out, but he always returned.

Inside the apartment the biker kicked off his boots and jeans, coated with dust from the construction site, and showered. He glanced at the burn on the inside of his arm where the welding rod had marked him that morning. His foreman had told him he was a fucking idiot to work in short sleeves. Then he'd gone off on a rant that all welders were fucking idiots anyway, so what the hell. The biker had only raised his goggles and stared in return, slow creases at the corners of his eyes.

The burn was crescent-shaped, a swollen, blistered sickle that smarted under the hot water. Steam and water and the shudder of worn pipes as the pressure increased. The biker leaned his head back under the flow and held his breath. One minute. More. He thought of the girl. Her hair like sorrow, long and sweeping; her mouth a muse, if only she kept quiet. She would though. He knew she would.

At a table by the window, a mother scolded her child. The girl wiped down a table nearby and tried not to listen. As she coupled the salt and pepper and turned to see the child looking into his lap, she couldn't help but remember. A late afternoon ten years before. Her own mother. The screaming.

"Your fucking paramours!" Her mother's voice had ripped through the house, a siren undone, no longer warning, sending only high hysterical messages. Her footsteps across the floor. Her arms flailing, knocking things over, trying to find more room when there was no room left.

Silence, then a murmur. Quiet words growing louder. Her father's voice tipping, without the balance it once had. "Right, darling." The endearment slurred and caustic. "I see you're not offering. Really though, given the opportunities, there's still not a single wife in this house to fuck."

And her mother. "You are unbelievable. How are we even standing here in the same room?" Her high heels striking the oak floors; her speech cut from the finest cloth, smooth and weighted, like elegant drapes. "It's not a matter of physics, of how two bodies rub together. It's about not giving a damn. You have no qualms, no guilt. No respect for our life. It's not just your life, you know."

And her father. No reply. Instead, an emptiness. The house filling up with stillness and breath and uncertainty. The girl imagined his eyes cast down, his shoulders hunched, his soft anger curling at the edges like a leaf of paper caught in flame. Whatever ashy trace remained might linger, the desperate smell of smoke hanging about for a long time.

She stood alone at the dresser in her bedroom, a seven-year-old in the dark. The door was open, and she saw the hallway wallpaper reflected in the dresser's mirror. Her image was indistinct, but out in the hall the pattern of stars, muted red stars, dwarfed by a blank white background, vibrated bright and apparent. She knew that at the center of each star a cross stood out, surrounded by sharp diagonal lines. Starbursts. The wallpaper was aged, as tired as her mother. The girl leaned in toward her reflection and saw her mother ascending the stairs, running past her doorway down the hall. Everything had changed. The girl understood this and followed her mother, but then paused, the threadbare runner under her feet. In the west window the sun was going down, its last blushing light a lie.

As the years went by, she realized that her mother had blamed her father, who couldn't keep his hands to himself and tried out literature students like the new and immodest words in his plays. Seniors, freshman, men, women. The paramours. Without discretion or discrimination. And so he'd lost his job. And his wife. But he still had his daughter. The girl knew that she should be angry with him, but she couldn't find a way. Sometimes bitterness landed like a pound of pennies at the back of her throat, and she would lock herself in the bathroom, choking and crying. But her father's sad face swept away the anger.

Lately, on the nights when he was home, they watched old films together. *Rebecca, It Happened One Night, The Thin Man.* They repeated Nick and Nora's lines at the breakfast table, he Nick, she Nora. *Nick: "I'm a hero. I was shot twice in the Tribune." Nora: "I read where you were shot five times in the tabloids." Nick: "It's not true. He didn't come anywhere near my tabloids."* And they laughed. Rarely, he took her to Miss Mae's, the corner bar, where he drank too much and attempted to teach her to handle a pool cue with passion, to aim the darts with ease.

Now the girl took a five-minute break to call her father. She leaned against the wall and stretched the phone cord, twisting it around her fingers. "I'll be home late, okay?" A buzz through the line; static. "I'm going out with friends. It's Wednesday. Nothing else to do. What do you care anyway, right? I just wanted to let you know." A pause; a click. "Daddy?" she said to the empty line. "I just wanted you to know."

At seven o'clock it was still light outside. The world had a pearl look to it, the clouds and sky. It spoke rain. Here, rain was always spoken. Humidity, heat. Dull river winds, if any. Fog, mist, eventual rain.

Along the river's bend, business was good at the café that had recently opened. Outside tables were full; diners seemed satisfied with the enormous salads and homemade breads; the evening waitresses were there already, casually taking orders. Across the avenue, on the neutral ground, a streetcar edged around the curved tracks. A crow browsed at the streetcar stop for litter—crumbs, cigarette butts, bits of sticky waxed paper. Above, live oak branches were swathed in Spanish moss. Below, a black Harley, its lines sleek and definite, was parked curbside by the café.

The girl stepped out of the front doors laughing, her long hair gathered in a high swinging ponytail. She wore jeans and a frayed white t-shirt which read, across the slight rise of her chest, "bamboozled" in bold, black letters. She was tall, almost taller than the biker who followed her, and her gait was young and uneven, while his carried a strange elegance, a surety in direction that hers did not yet have. His shirtsleeves had been rolled up on his forearms, and his hand brushed the girl's waist as he guided her along the sidewalk to the curb where the motorcycle waited.

Two helmets hung alongside the bike. He handed her the red one, and as she put it on, he held her hips, then kissed her. They lingered under the trees like that. Another streetcar went by, this time in the opposite direction. And then they were astride the leather seat, the Harley engine heavy with bass as they rode off—the black and red helmets, the white of her shirt a blur against the street corner—away from the avenue and down the river road.

She thought she would love the wind. Instead, it puzzled and unsettled her. It whipped inside the open helmet, tearing at her hair. Trees blurred by; a few cars swept past, quick and indistinct. She tried not to breathe for there was too much wind at once. The immediacy of the ride startled her, and she tried to relax, to just let it happen. The girl closed her eyes and then opened them. She reached forward and glanced the biker's arm. He held out his wrist to her, and above it she saw the crescent-shaped burn. Sunset pushed color over the levee, and she thought of roses and camellias and dying red stars.

The day after her parents had fought, it had rained. The girl had stood beside her father, watching him make breakfast. Before her, the cast-iron skillet, sizzling bacon, the gas flame wavering. With her bare hand she held onto the handle, not letting go until her father moved her so suddenly that she cried out. Her mother had left that morning, all bags, no goodbyes; and so the girl stood at the kitchen sink, her father holding her hand under the cold faucet water, her palm streaked with white, at first numb and then throbbing. Later, she hadn't been able to grasp her brush and had to ask her father to pull her hair back for school.

And now there wasn't even a scar, just a faded outline, a memory of that morning. She showed the biker her palm, the center slightly darker than the surrounding area, and he held her hand gently, then let it go. She traced the biker's forearm and wondered but didn't ask about the burn, its clean curved shape.

As they passed the edges of Black Pearl, the Baptist church doors open for Wednesday night service, the sky opened up, clouds lit with apricot light. Her mother's gardener had once lived in this part of town. The girl wondered if he was still alive; he had been so old and gnarled even before her mother left. Her father asked him not to come back after the time he'd trimmed the Japanese Plum tree, and he said, of course, he understood. Every winter the plums littered the yard, leaving a sweet stench, and the garden had grown wild, the roses climbing over the garage, the camellias bleak and faded.

Now the girl was seventeen, and at dusk the mosquitoes still arrived in droves, the air a murmur of gauzed wings, the view murky and vague. In three months she would graduate from high school. Her straight A's would be enough. Tip money from the café might be enough. She needed to leave before it was too late. Before her father begged her not to go. Like her mother. Before she knew she had to stay. Maybe the biker would take her to Texas or Florida, or to a state without mosquitoes, without beautiful sunsets.

She wrapped her arms around him and felt the breadth of his ribcage and the textured cotton of his shirt. When the bike angled sideways into a curve, she experienced the curve through his body: assured, calm, in charge. She realized they were heading away from town, crossing from Orleans into Jefferson Parish where the houses and shops leaned against each other. Tired, compact little buildings. Resting her hands above the biker's belt buckle, the girl gathered herself, breathing in and out, as though she were entitled to this moment, to whatever came next.

For a second the biker took one hand off the handlebar and found her hands. His touch was warm as he pulled one of her hands to his lips, resting it there, holding it like a small bird protected from the wind. And then he slowed the bike, the motor emitting a low growl, and pulled into a side road lined with oyster shells.

She was all legs and innocence as she dismounted the bike. With her knee she grazed the worn seat and the winged emblem, chrome blackened with road dirt. The same hand he had held before he took now to help her balance, but she needed no help. He noticed her poise, the length of her stride, how she accepted his invitation. Just at her brow, a dark line from the helmet. He placed his thumb against the line and traced its sad meaning. Her hair had fallen and tangled during the ride; she tried to brush it through her fingers, almost apologetically.

She followed the biker, his lavender shirt, to the door. "I didn't know we'd come here first."

The biker stepped back so that she could enter. "Sometimes an evening is too short," he said, nearly whispering, as she walked through the threshold. "Why not live it backwards?"

She stood in the dark room with her back to the biker, the depth of the room's blackness, her eyes unaccustomed to its pitch, causing her to panic. His hand reached under her shirt, his palm at her waist, her stomach, her ribcage. The room smelled of cigarettes and incense. A hollow silence surrounded her. Somehow this was not what she had imagined. Now the room tilted slightly, and she realized the biker was holding her, carrying her.

"Now where?" she said.

The biker's breath came over her like cardamom, vetiver, cloves.

He felt her stiffen and then relax. He laid her on the bed, his hand grazing her throat, her breasts, the zipper of her jeans. He heard her sigh.

A flame. His lighter. A candle. The edges of the room grew brighter, and the sweet unmistakable smell of grass, lit and burning, fell upon her. His mouth over hers, his hands cupped close; she inhaled.

He kissed her and stood. She leaned up on her elbows and watched as he placed an album on the stereo, thin orange lines lighting up the receiver, the sound of a needle on vinyl, scratching slightly. Guitar edged out slowly, then drums and electric guitar. A resonant, bottomless sound. The biker held the joint like a cigarette all the while, wearing it down to nothing, and the girl lay back onto the bed. Inside the music she heard a voice as familiar as breakfasts with her father.

1969. The year after her mother had left. Standing outside of Butterfly Records, waiting for her father, she'd watched as her mother drove by. She knew it was her. Alone in a Mustang with a white vinyl roof. Smoking a cigarette, her long lovely arm against the door, the driver's window wide open.

The girl had run toward the street, but a Volkswagen whining in second gear had blocked her path. By then the Mustang had turned the corner, and only the taillights reflected back in the noon sun. At home her father played his new album, listening to the final song of side one over and over.

And now in this room, in this biker's bed, the same singer, a different song. Sweet and misleading—like the biker, like her father, like the recorded voice and the memories it tossed back up.

Candlelight licks the walls, and the girl is glad she can't see the wallpaper. The biker's hands are caught in her hair; he is above her. Guitar chords progress like her fingers against his shirt buttons. *Hello, sweetness, in the dust.* The sound of the biker's breath is bright, and the girl feels his weight. Her clothes lie on the floor at the end of the bed. *Hello, girlfriend of my dreams. This is not the way it seems.*

She shifts under him, and he knows her age. She is young and willing and honest. He has read her the right way all along. From the space between the mattress and the box spring, he takes a knife. *Hello, glimmer in the sand.* He lays it next to the girl's head and remembers the road, how once he could never remain in one place for too long, how he'd traveled light, always alone. He imagines her on the back of his bike, the tight muscles of her abdomen against his broad back, her weight a whisper compared to other women he's had. How she might go with him if he again decided to leave. But the blade is silver and catches the light, distracting him.

The girl's eyes are closed and the biker kisses them. She holds his face and urges him with her hips. In the second before the knife touches, he watches her: how unfamiliar, how small her expression. He leans back and draws the blade to her throat. As the metal lies against her pale skin, she tilts her chin and he waits for her to cry. But she doesn't.

For a time he rests the blade there and she swallows, the cold metallic edge so unlike the voice, the singing, that reels in something old and warm out of the past, repeating itself over and over. Out of the past, there would always be questions. The rush and resilience of the moment of unknowing. But now there is the possibility of something else, imbalanced and imperfect, no better than distance and dying stars.

Like that, the biker measures the girl, all the while caressing her, his blade shining like her eyes, now open, still accepting whatever might come.

ELIZA, IN THE EVENT OF A HURRICANE

When your sister, Eliza, stands in front of the TV dressed in her rain gear and shrimping boots with hands on hips, get out the masking tape. El will fiddle with the volume control and stare at the screen and then shout, "This is going to be a good one!" Once she does this, it will be clear that the tropical storm has become a true hurricane. At the end of August, this is nothing to question. Start taping the windows with wide X's and pray for rain over wind, though you know you'll get both.

As soon as El changes the channel from Angela Hill to Anderson Cooper, you're sure things have gone from bad to worse. Fill the bathtub to the brim, but don't add any Epsom salts. You may have to drink the stuff later. Last time the tub water lasted only five days, and you needed five weeks' worth.

Saturday nights are not usually like this. Usually, they involve setting out to the bayou to hear the tree frogs carry on; or to listen while the Des Allemands cousins, Nicolette and Bobbie Renoir, scratch out some *chansons* on their fiddles; or to chase Eliza one more time down Highway 1, as she heads to Dufrene Building Materials in Cut Off to find her beau.

That beau was a mistake. Wielded a power saw in the *You-Order-It-We'll-Trim-It* department and said, offhand and over a length of cypress board, he was headed for Hollywood. Said to watch for him on television, that he'd be there any day now. Instead, there was Eliza standing one aisle over in *Home*

Security, staring through the stacks of hardware, looking for a way in. But there was no way into that man's soul. Instead of a soul, he had a lockbox, and it was locked up tight. No key, no way. And he never did show up on TV. Not even on a Saturday night.

On this particular night we get weathermen, talking and talking. And when El pulls the ottoman up to the television, it becomes evident that you're in this for the long haul. She looks at you and winks and cracks the same joke she told five minutes before. Something about a girl walking into a warehouse where nobody works and nothing is sold. Smile, but don't laugh.

In the kitchen tear open several packages of Camellia red beans, cover them with water in your tallest cooking pot, and set them on the stove. Turn the flame up high: there's no time for soaking them now. Get to the fridge and pull out a six-pack, hand a beer to El and crack open another for yourself.

El won't even glance up, but she'll take a long draw, reminding you of last time, when the case of Dixie lasted through hardly half of the marathon broadcast of *Arrested Development.* Convinced that actor Will Arnett, aka "Gob," bore a striking resemblance to her beau and most probably was her beau finally gone off to Hollywood in order to reveal his talent in millions of megapixels, El nearly lost her mind when the power went down. Remember how you'd wished for more beer, for a handful of Valium, for a better way. Then consider a trip to Liberto's, just around the corner, even though every last beer will be long gone.

When El starts dancing in place because of all the beer she's drunk, promise her that you'll keep a watch over the radar screen until she returns. She mouths something at you about the northeast longitude picking up where the southeast latitude left off. Down the hall she yells, "That was where I met him!" This reminds you of a song which you've been trying to forget.

Once you hear the flush and the sound of her rubber boots on the linoleum, back away from the TV set. In the center of the screen, a churning white spiral moves over the Gulf, and the memory of the waves and the wind makes you sit down. As rain slams sideways into the taped windows and a low-pressure moan encircles the house, the earth sinks underneath you and then turns in another direction. El runs back into the room and yells, "What the hell are you doing just sitting there?"

Shake your head and repeat slowly to yourself, "non, non, non," then cross yourself, "au nom du Père, le Fils, et le Saint-Esprit." St. Mary's Assumption is already boarded up, so consign yourself to the kitchen and search out your largest cast iron. Fill it with oil and butter, onions and garlic, celery and green peppers, and the spiciest Andouille. Let them cook down and say a prayer to

St. Valérie. Be thankful that you no longer live in Thibodaux, that there are enough candles and batteries.

Consider how even as a little girl, Eliza loved tropical depressions, white caps out on the Gulf, the satellite gaze of a spiraling storm. From the window seat up on the stair landing, she would sit and call for hurricanes by name, even the ones that were born before she was—Hazel and Hattie, Audrey and Dora. At seven years old, she lit all the hurricane lanterns before the electricity went out, and the aunts sighed, "mon Dieu," and ran around the house to blow them out. Only moments later Camille left us standing around in darkness, Eliza laughing behind her hands. Back then, she was convinced that eventually her name would be chosen and her own storm would swoop down and carry her away.

At twelve, at the height of a Category 4 called Carmen, Eliza opened all the windows, and we had to sweep the oak leaves and twigs out onto the porch before we could even mop up. She watched us twisting the mop tails into buckets and said, "I only wanted to see her coming." At seventeen, incensed that the National Hurricane Center had decided to introduce men's names to their Atlantic and Gulf lists, she took off for the beach and ended up on a roof in Biloxi, roped onto a chimney with complete strangers.

Shake your head again and add the softened red beans into the cast iron along with a ham bone and watch them settle against the brown and gold and fading green of the other ingredients. Remember how you used to settle against your little sister, back when it was easy for her to sit still and accept your company. Now, in the next room, El sets up a hand of solitaire across the ottoman, queens outnumbering kings.

At the back door check the sky outside. Wonder why the stars are out. Wonder how the moon could possibly think of waning while there are waves as big as houses crashing over Grand Isle. Wonder if this hurricane will be as much of a bitch as Betsy.

Watch El sleeping cross-legged on the floor with her head slung over a pair of jacks and three kings. The queens all lie face down on the floor. Turn them face up and pause at the queen of hearts' resemblance to El. Remember the time she was pitched over the olives and nuts at the Saturn Bar by the accordionist from Lafitte, when she turned up the volume on the TV during his set. Hurricane Frances was raging over Florida and El just needed to get a better idea of her northerly direction.

Outside, the wind picks up and you know the eye has passed over, that the next ring of weather will soon be leaning into your little shotgun house. By the time this storm has turned east toward Mississippi or west toward Texas, your sister may be awake. She may push her dark hair from her face and look up at you. She may smell the red beans and know that they are ready.

She'll pull the curtains back and a notice the rain is diminishing. And she'll walk over to the television and turn it off. Gaze at her and consider all the hurricanes in your lives, grateful that, so far, you've both survived them all.

ONE NIGHT, ONE AFTERNOON,
SOONER OR LATER

In the uptown Canal Villere, we are standing in front of the wine shelf, looking for the Bolla Valpolicella. We aren't pushing a grocery cart because our needs are basic, our pockets thin with dollar bills and change. It's late on a Saturday night and we've nothing better to do. Micah says his brother's out of town, so we can go to his apartment and watch movies. Jude has already walked to the checkout and is picking out a soft pack of Camels. We are all bored, and so we smoke too much.

Outside, the night is drenched in New Orleans's wavering city lights. Above are clouds of muted lavender and copper. I reach out to touch the sky and realize the drugs are already working. We fly down Claiborne Avenue with the Volkswagen's top down. Jude likes to drive fast, and we pass everyone else on the road. I watch from the backseat as people in Monte Carlos and Mustangs blur past, and my eyes start to sting and tear.

"Slow down, Jude," I yell.

"No way, sister." He takes a corner, and the VW seems to lift sideways for a moment.

Then again, maybe it's the drugs.

I have no clue what I've taken. Something dark and sinister that's filling me up with a strange purple feeling. I slide down in the seat even though we've arrived.

"Come on," Jude says.

He seems impatient and looks down at me. I love his dark hair, his dark-

41

er eyes. He reaches into the back and offers me his hand. In his other hand is a lit cigarette. Like I said, we are bored, in that long summer stretch, that limbo between semesters, and this is just one way to skip through another evening.

We've been spending too much time together. Micah with his Gibson and his Dylan imitations, Jude joining in with a second guitar, me just sitting and listening, not bothering to understand the lyrics. Laughing. The three of us, a habit. Impetuous and willful and wanting to push limits, or each other, whichever comes first.

I grab Jude's hand. I love his hands. They are strong, wicked elegant, capable hands. And he nearly lifts me right out of the car. I climb the last bit and end up in the street on my ass. Micah gazes down at me.

"Sitting on the pavement thinking about the government?"

The sloped road is making me feel lopsided and out of sorts. "What do you think?" I say back.

"Look out, kid." He takes the bag of wine and leaves me there.

Yet again, I'm sitting in the street. I think I've been in this same spot before. There are oyster shell fragments and gravel and bits of debris around me, and I don't feel like getting up. Jude shouts at me to get the fuck up. Since he's not helping, I pull myself up by holding onto the car door handle. I love my Volkswagen, white and shiny with little silver door handles.

Soon I'm standing in front of the brother's place. Micah's brother. I wonder if his eyes are as wide and swimming as Micah's. It's an upstairs apartment with an outdoor stairway. I step out of my shoes and onto the smooth tile steps, each tile a slightly different color—red, orange, brown. I am so damned quiet in my bare feet. Micah is behind me. His hands are on my waist. His mouth just barely touches the back of my neck. But I'm Jude's girl, so this is different. Micah's breath is warm, and Jude is already upstairs. I follow the stairway around, the iron railing under my palm, guiding me. Micah is no longer there. He has stopped to pick up my shoes.

Inside, the TV's on. *Saturday Night Live.* Bill Murray and Jane Curtin are being rude to each other, and I stand in the doorway, watching their faces twist, listening to their voices curl. Eric Idle is the host. I love Eric Idle, and suddenly I'm laughing without even knowing I'm laughing until I almost spill the wine that's somehow in my hand. Jude is lying on the couch, and now I'm sitting on the floor below him. I don't remember this glass of wine, but it's red and it's in my hand. And Micah's somewhere. Is Micah somewhere? Yes, there he is, in the chair over there, and he's looking at me. I take a sip of wine and look back at him. Jude watches the show, and Roseanne Roseannadanna makes him laugh out loud. I wish I could do the same thing. Make Jude laugh.

Yesterday on the way to Des Allemands, Jude yelled at me from his truck.

We were shooting down Carrollton Avenue to I-10, Jude in his truck and Micah and me in the VW. I was smoking a cigarette, hanging my arm out the Volkswagen window, and Jude was alongside us, shouting and pointing. I guess Micah had forgotten to put the gas cap back on after he filled up at the Texaco. I pulled my arm inside the car and put the cigarette out. Why we were going out to the bayou at noon I didn't really understand. Micah and Jude thought it was a good idea and had even bought turkey necks that morning.

For some reason Jude was driving his truck, the crabbing nets and a cooler of ice and beer all loaded in back, and we were following in the VW with the turkey necks in a bag under my feet. It was only when Jude yelled at me about the cigarette and the gas cap and blowing the fuck up that I wondered about taking two cars. Since he'd begged so much, I'd even let Micah drive.

Roseanne Roseannadanna is not making me laugh. She keeps trying to touch Jane Curtin's nose, and Jude reaches over now and touches mine. He likes to do this. I guess he thinks it's nice. I haven't ever said so, but it's annoying. Or is it just that my sense of humor is being sucked away? This wine is too red and too dry and it's making me want to drink more.

Micah gets up and goes into the kitchen. He brings back three glasses of water. He sets one down next to a half full ashtray, then hands me one. How did he know that I was thirsty?

I accidentally spill a little onto my legs, and it's cold. Micah drinks his water until it's gone, gone, gone. He has this light brown wavy hair and he's real skinny. Too much speed, not enough grits. Or something. He motions to Jude, who has fallen asleep. Jude was just laughing, so how can he be asleep? *Saturday Night Live* is over, and an old black-and-white film is throwing light out into the room. Time is on its own, shiftless.

I try to remember the day before. How by two in the afternoon, I'd felt done. Done with the hot sun, the tepid brown water of Bayou Gauche, the bare spot we'd found, no shade at all. Micah in the only tree around, small and nearly limbless. On the shore opposite, huge cypresses were littered with sleeping white egrets. I kept thinking how cool it looked over there, and Micah kept yelling about the turkey necks. Jude checked the lines, pulling them up very slowly, and managed to net seven blue crabs. They were sizeable and pissed off too. Inside the ice chest they clattered around until cold enough not to care.

Nobody else was out there; nobody else was stupid enough to go crabbing in the midday, mid-July heat. They were all inside, sitting in front of giant electric fans and drinking iced teas.

I am stupid enough, though. I go wherever the boys go. We are inseparable, a trio, twisted together, trying to figure things out by doing them, by not doing them.

Micah is sitting next to me now. Jude is above us on the couch, talking in his sleep. Is he really asleep? Or is he asking us what the fuck we're doing? Micah slides his hand under my shirt. His hand is smaller than Jude's. He bites his nails and looks worried a lot. Sometimes he sounds like Dylan. *Blonde on Blonde* Dylan. *Highway 61* Dylan. But now he sounds like nobody I've ever met, his breath like a freight train inside my ear.

"Come on," Micah says.

I realize this is the second time I've heard this tonight.

"What?" I say.

"So useless and all," Jude says. He is still asleep and turns away, his face to the back of the couch, his back to us. He is so long; his legs go forever. The couch is corduroy, and I think of how his face will be imprinted with vertical stripes when he finally wakes.

"Come on," Micah says again. He is a little boy lost, his voice small and hollow, and this time the request has a different meaning.

"Where?" I answer. The living room looks lilac, and the TV is blue. There is one lamp on, but it's in a different room. Which room?

Micah is pulling me off the floor and I must weigh a million pounds. He's got me up now and we're going toward that light. Before we get there, he stops and I lean against a wall and he cups my face with his small hands and there's that breath all over again. Micah has incredible breath, sweet and warm, like cinnamon and chocolate. I let him kiss me, even though somewhere in the back of my mind, there's a little niggling that feels lonesome and wrong. The kiss is undeveloped, a precious thing, and I feel it working on me, undoing my spine. And then I realize it's Micah's fingers undoing the buttons down the back of my blouse.

The niggling grows as the buttons unbutton. Still, I don't try to stop Micah and eventually he pulls my blouse off. I look down at it. On the floor. In a small gauzy heap.

At Bayou Gauche the afternoon sun bleached the mud bank the color of dirty china. The crabs kept coming. Jude lowered the lines one by one and tied them off onto the railing of the little bridge we'd come across. I sat at one end and watched him, the white line silent, his hands moving, his fingers quick but the entire movement gradual. Slow motion. That's how he loved me most times. In slow motion. He glanced at me now and then and smiled.

Micah was still off in his tree, singing. The words were loud and then soft, like his gaze could be. Mean, defiant; then lulled. As usual, he was channeling Dylan. "But I would not feel so all alone," he yelled. He wanted what he wanted and if he couldn't have it, he cried.

The sun was hot and wretched on my shoulders, and I wished for a wide-brimmed hat. My can of beer was half empty and warm, my cigarettes almost gone. I squinted back at Micah, then over at Jude. I was an in-between girl, and those boys were waiting, just waiting, to see what I'd do.

"Lors," Micah says.

"Lors," Jude says, still facing the back of the couch.

Micah looks over his shoulder, then back at me. I see the lamp now, and it's in a bedroom. Micah is sleepy-eyed and pulling me that way. I see a bed and resist. A girl in nothing but cut-off jeans and resisting.

"What?" Micah says, smiling, trying to draw me in.

"No," I say. I undo my wrist from his hand, but not without twisting it free.

"Why not?"

I scoop up my blouse and hold it up to my bare chest.

"Why the hell not?" Micah has turned into mean Micah.

I try to put on my blouse and he tears it out of my hands. A button pops off and clicks as it hits the hardwood floor. It lays there, a glistening thing, like an open eye.

"Why?" he says.

"Micah, just stop."

"Sooner or later," he says. He nearly sings. He pushes me into the bedroom and grabs the back of my hair, right at the nape, right where it hurts.

The bed has a white spread over it and the lamplight washes it whiter. Still holding onto my hair with one hand, Micah grasps me around the waist with the other. He's kissing my throat, and I wait. I'm not uninterested; I'm certainly not uninvolved. I just want to see what happens. Micah loosens his hold when I stop struggling. I give in and find a place outside of myself; in that moment I become the yes-girl. But the lamp is too bright, and I reach over and turn it off.

First light seeps through the windows above. Gray, uncertain, unpredictable. Barely a color, barely there. That sad time when night gives into day, when I haven't slept enough and wish for just a few more hours of darkness. But now Micah is over me, kissing my naked breasts. I know this is wrong and still I lie there, letting him. Letting him. Even with Jude in the next room. I sit up and kiss him back. And then I push him away.

"That's all," I say.

He starts to cry. I knew he would.

The crabs were a stunning sight, gray-blue backs with aqua legs and claws, outlined in magenta. We had seventeen in the ice chest before we realized that Micah was delirious. He'd been drinking beer and was red-faced and crazy-looking.

"You're not my mother!" he screamed at me. "You're not my sister!" And louder still, "You're not even my lover!"

"No, I'm not," I said. "And I'm driving. You're wasted and it's my car, dammit."

Jude and I carried the chest between us, the top barely closed, mostly full of big busters. And then Jude had to go back for Micah, who wouldn't get out of the tree. I couldn't see past the dull green marsh grasses and stood in the bed of the truck for a better view.

Micah swatted at Jude, who was much taller and stronger and avoided Micah's little slaps. "You go your way and I'll go mine," Micah yelled. "I'm gonna let you pass, you son of a—" He tried to cling to the tree and climb higher, but there was no more tree to climb.

In the end Jude had to trick him and pry him loose and sling him over his shoulder. Micah's hair flopped around and he shouted obscure things, more at the dirt than at Jude or me. He called us lousy film stars and '60s wannabes and misfits and dullards. "Time will tell," he half-shouted, half-moaned. Jude told him to shut the fuck up.

On the way home Micah fell asleep in the back seat of the VW. I followed Jude's F-150, the right taillight still busted out from the time Micah kicked it. By the time we reached Kenner, the bright orange sun fell to one side of Lake Pontchartrain, leaving the rest of the way home muted and tinged with pink streaks and just a little bit of despair. The summer was halfway over, and the world beyond the bayou seemed to me an uneven, unrelenting sort of place. And I didn't know how much longer I wanted to be there.

SWEET IOWA

The first time Howdy Miller saw Morgan Loving she was walking across the barroom, her legs like scissors cutting up the room, slicing through the stares that followed her. She had the kind of walk that would take her somewhere. Howdy didn't wonder where she'd been, just where she was going, as if the future might lengthen her stride. Her blouse fit close to her waist and was detailed with some sort of blue flowers. Bachelor buttons? Prairie asters? She wore it tucked into her jeans. Dark, new, slightly stiff—they whispered when she walked.

The fellows at the pool table stopped their game, looking up to watch her, and then someone made a shot, the white cue ball cracking a bright red into the side pocket. Men's laughter, a sportscast droning from the television above the bar, Merle Haggard singing from the jukebox. Here and around town, Howdy had heard Morgan Loving was a west Texas girl. Young, lean, strong, blown in from the mile-high desert between Marfa and Odessa.

Howdy slowly drank a whisky and followed her direction—assured, unlike his own lopsided gait, that one leg slightly shorter than the other. Marking the way she crossed the room, her body angled forward, the slight waver in one ankle, the bend of her knees, he felt a sudden sadness. It settled somewhere deep, fell like a pebble on water, not skipping, but sinking, leaving only an impression—a sense of relief—widening out on the surface of his mind. Though this calmed him, he knew the relief was false, so he let it go, and the sadness floated up again like the bobber on a fishing line.

Sweet Jesus, he thought.

He noticed her boots, tan and well worn, as she stepped up to the bar, and heard the bartender, Stran, call to her. "Hey there, Miss Loving. The usual?" She drank tequila. Threw her head straight back—a quick twist of her hand, the shot glass lit up like a spark, the green rind of a lime—taking each shot in a bare swallow.

From his seat in the corner booth, Howdy saw that she smoked Chesterfields. White trails flew around her as she waved her hands, telling the bartender a story. Something about a pig. She'd chosen a good place to be if she knew anything about pigs. Dynamo, Iowa, was covered in farmland, and pigs were second only to corn. Seemed she knew her breeds, how to choose high-grade stock. And then she let everyone know her intentions.

"Wake up, Stran. It's 1990." She pointed to the Tammy Wynette wall calendar from 1973. "I'm up here for good reason—to search out a pig that's right for tossing, then find a place to let it fly."

Stran Shirley laughed outright. Nearly knocked over the beer he shouldn't have been drinking. Owning a bar named *Shirley's* hadn't won him any love either. Still, the town drank there. And that afternoon they listened to him laugh and Morgan Loving shift from stories to near silence.

"You're that girl in the news, aren't you?" he said. "Guess I better watch myself."

"Good guess," she said, obviously not amused.

Stran looked as if he'd been dismissed early. "Well, now don't get mad, Miss Loving."

"Not a chance." She kicked her barstool backwards, threw down a handful of bills, and walked toward the door.

Once that door had slammed shut, Howdy Miller sat back in his booth and, for some strange and unspeakable reason, knew the earlier sadness he'd felt was unwinding into something like longing. Or was it something like love?

A spring storm front came through, with winds hard and unrelenting that lasted for days. The cornfields lay fallow, and dried stalks whipped around in the restless air. The old barn shuddered and let in drafts, and last season's hay blew about the loft. Howdy sat below in a rusted garden chair. Spread out before him were parts of a tractor engine, disassembled, waiting to be cleaned or reworked or replaced: cylinder sleeves, piston gauges and rings, gaskets, sparkplugs, bearings, and a grease-stained Allis Chalmers manual. A blackened rag across his knees, Howdy worked at a rusted plug with a steel-wired brush. The brush had almost been worn down to nothing; still, it had some worth and he would keep using it until the bristles were completely gone.

It was a Sunday, spread with too much time, and he kept busy so as not to think of Morgan Loving. In the past weeks, she'd become a sweet drifting thought, one that caught him off guard, and he knew she'd remain just that—a thought, far-off and unreachable. Howdy Miller was a simple farmer, born Howard Everett Miller III in 1960 and raised on his family's pig farm. He knew very little of women, the girls in school shying away from the boy with the limp, not bad looking, but awkward and on his own most of the time. He had no sisters, and his mother allowed his father to care for him. She'd cooked and cleaned but was neither interested in farm work nor her only child and sent him off with his father to do morning chores, to catch the bus to school, and out to the fields or pond every afternoon. Even the fact that he'd been born off-kilter gave her no sway to love him more. Perhaps for this reason, Howdy had been wary of women—until now.

During his weekday rounds of the pig barns, he had grown morose and went through his days deep in thought. He was certain the AG students doing research on his breeds didn't mind or even notice the change in his mood; normally, he was quiet anyway. The livestock fell to their corn with the usual ambition: the grunting, the rooting and pushing that was typical of pigs in spring. He studied the breeds, and—though fascinated with their markings, the slight differences in snout shape and the flip of their ears, and the way they spoke out in deep mutterings or thin-pitched squeals—he never felt an attachment.

Throughout the long swine barns, he oversaw the care of Large Whites, Yorkshires, Berkshires, Old Spots, Tamworths, even the rare American Mulefoot. Old Man Stipes—Emmett Croswell Stipes—had left his farm to the town of Dynamo, with the firm recommendation that it stay in the hands of the Miller family. The Millers held the land that bordered his, and more importantly, they knew pigs. Down through the generations, everything the Millers did was in the name of pigs, and Stipes's last will and testament held a clause that retained his farm as one for swine and swine only. The farm was now associated with the state university's agricultural program, and Howdy had become more sought out by the AG students than the professors who taught genetics and addressed behavior and breeding issues from a scientific standpoint.

A few days earlier, he'd noticed a small male Tamworth who had taken to standing by himself in one corner of the pen. The other males were widening out, the ribcages stippled with fat and muscle, their coarse coats practical and golden under the barn's interior lights. Leaner than any of the other swine breeds, the Tamworths were still boisterous. They bumped against each other and looked about, always alert to the possibility of more feed.

The little fellow, however, stood quite still. His color seemed a paler gold than his brothers' and his demeanor was oddly human. It was as though he'd just been scolded and stood alone out of shame. Howdy considered the pig. He opened the gate to the pen, then pushed through the Tams with the wooden crook he always carried and tapped the quiet pig forward and out of the pen. Once in the aisleway, the small Tamworth didn't try to bolt and remained motionless. He sniffed the air in front of him. Then, when prodded with the wooden crook, he moved along at a trot, his head up and attentive.

Howdy followed him, the bum leg that had kept him out of wars and away from women stiffening his walk. Even in the barn, the seep of chill March air went straight through his Carhartts. The pig nosed along each pen, and the animals inside bumped and grunted in response. At the end of the aisle, the pig turned, held his nose up, and sniffed once more. From twenty feet away, he seemed almost dapper. He was a runt, but one that was just too curious and spry to worry over. He'd never make bacon, but he would surely be useful for something. Back in his pen, he faced the corner again.

Later that evening, twilight approaching, Howdy stopped again at long barn # 2. The evening was pitched with a dark, cloudless sky and the wind kept changing directions. He pulled at the high barn door, and it scraped open along the warped runners. Under the dim overheads, the pigs were mostly asleep, huddled together, some lying on their wide sides. Standing once more at the center pen, Howdy looked down at the little Tamworth. His back end was muddy, and his tail bent into a relaxed sort of curl. He seemed to be asleep, but he was still standing and alone, away from the mass of brothers lumped one next to the other.

Without thinking much about the AG students' research and the possible consequences of one less Tamworth head to count, Howdy silently entered the pen, hoisted the half-sized pig, and walked slowly out of the barn. The Tam was quiet, somehow unsurprised at the whole event, but not without interest. When set down on the cracked vinyl seat of the pickup, he gazed out the window. To Howdy, it seemed he was wishing the place farewell.

Now, in the old Miller barn, his hands dark with grease from the work on the tractor engine, Howdy felt a combination of calm and despair. The little pig was stalled nearby, his rough murmurings like a sweet salve to the farmer's unease. Life was too long to live alone, and while he considered the animal worthy of company, the fellow was hardly the same as the woman that called up all his quietly unsettled attention these days. Still, he'd given the creature a name, the same one that ran across the signboard of the long barn: Emmett Croswell Stipes. The old man was certainly tossing about in his grave, and perhaps with this in mind, Howdy spoke softly to the pig, calling him "Emmett" and "Em."

Outside the wind grappled with something metal, and inside a line of fishing poles trembled as the building shook. There was a shrill coiling noise: a car in need of a new fan belt coming up the drive. Then a door slammed, and a voice called out, thin and tapering, nearly diminished. A blast of wind hit the barn.

"Hello… Dammit! Jesus H, is anybody here?" She muscled through the old weathered door, which the wind held closed. "Hey!"

There was Morgan Loving, with a milder drift in her voice than Howdy had heard at *Shirley's*. She stood in the barn entrance, holding the door just wide enough to slip through, the late afternoon sky strange and gray-green behind her.

Howdy stood up, set the brush and spark plug on the seat, and tried unsuccessfully to wipe the black from his hands.

"Are you Howard Miller?" she asked. Her hair was loose and darker than he remembered.

"I am," he said slowly. "Howdy to most."

"Well, I'm Morgan. Morgan Loving."

Howdy exhaled, a thread of revelation traveling his spine, and released a soft, scraping trough-like sound. Ignoring what must have seemed a tone of consternation or bewilderment, the girl approached him and tried to shake his hand. He showed her a blackened palm and shrugged.

"Nice to meet you," Howdy said, though the phrase felt as worn-out to him as the low rasp which was his voice.

"I understand you know all about pigs," she said. There was indeed something new, something softer in her attitude.

"Well, I suppose it's true." He held the rag between his hands, trying not to wring it. "I seem to have landed that way."

"Landed," she said. "Funny, I'm looking for a pig to do just that."

He tried to understand her, and then stopped trying. It was enough just to gaze.

"I'm looking for a pig."

"Right."

He walked past her, stopping in front of the low stall where Emmett dozed. Morgan followed him and peered over the rough-boarded wall at the Tamworth. For a moment she was quiet, just staring. Then she looked straight at Howdy, and he saw her eyes were wide-set and two different colors, one green and one brown.

"Tell me," he said, "why do you need a pig? Are you doing research?"

She laughed at this, loud and long. "Research!" she said. "That's good, Howdy. That's real good. You are too funny." She studied him straight on again. "Tell me, how'd you get that nickname?"

"Oh, you know," he began. "The usual way."

The pig was sitting up now and grunted in a satisfied way.

"Oh, lord!" Morgan said. "Would you look at that? It's like he's watching us."

Howdy continued watching her. "He does that," he said. "Listen, would you like something to drink?"

"What are you offering?"

"Well, I can make coffee back at the house."

"Get real, Howdy."

The sweater she wore bunched around her hips and her jacket bit at her waist, an unopened pack of cigarettes edging from a side pocket. She bent over to stroke Emmett, and Howdy noticed her long legs once more. She was younger than he'd realized.

He turned, walked over to the workbench, and opened the cupboard above. A dust-covered bottle of Old Crow sat on the shelf next to rusted paint cans and empty Mason jars. He pulled it out, along with a pair of jars. When he turned around, Morgan was lifting Emmett out of the stall. A bare bulb of light cast an unusual yellow glow over them. Morgan held the pig aloft, seeming to size him up, and then grasped him as though she might pitch him across the barn.

Emmett was a good fifty pounds, and Morgan was no shirking daisy to lift him that way. It dizzied Howdy to see her holding him up as if he were a prize or part of some strange blessing. The glass jars clinked together in his hands, and Morgan turned his way.

"Nice pig," she said.

"Yes," Howdy answered. "A fine pig, just a bit small." He set down the jars and poured a good measure of whisky into each.

Morgan put Emmett down and clucked her tongue at him. When she walked over to Howdy, the pig followed. Why, thought Howdy, had she come on this night of all nights? Completely unfazed by the weather, she watched the little Tam over her shoulder.

"He's like a damned dog," she said and then laughed again, the sound cascading through the building. A sound that had never entered there. The sound of a woman laughing.

Howdy held out the whisky to her, and she smiled.

"All right then," she said, raising her jar. "To tossing a good pig!"

"I beg your pardon?" Howdy held onto his triple-aged Crow while she drank hers down.

"He's just the right size," Morgan answered.

"What are you talking about?" Howdy asked.

"You don't read the paper, do you? You really are all on your own out here." She glanced down at the dust and hay-strewn ground and then smiled. "Believe me, you don't need to know."

"Yes, I do." Howdy drank the whisky and considered her toast. Pig-tossing. Sounded foolish at best.

Morgan handed him the Mason jar. "More?" she asked.

He poured another measure. She sipped it this time. Below, Emmett nosed around their ankles, seemingly content.

"What are you really doing here?" Howdy said, suddenly tired.

"Prospecting," she said. And there was his answer.

They drove off in his truck—Howdy, Morgan, and the pig. It might have been the whisky, but Howdy was certain it was something stranger and more powerful that had made him agree. The evening had a tilt to it, and Howdy decided it was now or never for reeling in some of the mystery his life had been missing. As objectionable as pig-tossing sounded, he was also curious. Morgan promised that it was not inhumane, simply a gesture for those times when life seemed a little too slow. She promised that Emmett would be just fine.

Along the two-lane road a few miles outside of town, Stran Shirley's competitor had an establishment, a bar called *Lucille's*. The times he'd driven past, Howdy had never seen anyone but men enter. Morgan motioned for him to pull into the lot out front, and Howdy noticed how the old pickup stood out, large and ungainly, from the sleek chrome and leather of the motorcycles parked alongside.

Emmett nosed up against Morgan, and she patted his rough little back. "Now this goes quick," she said. "I'm talking lightning fast. Okay?"

Howdy regarded her dully.

"It's all about the element of surprise, Howdy," she went on.

How in the world had she talked him into this? He had only asked for an account, a few details, and now he was about to witness the event itself. He felt himself wavering, ready to set the truck in reverse and head back home.

Morgan lifted Emmett, slid off the seat onto the graveled parking surface, and strode to the front entrance. Howdy wasn't quick enough to open the door for her, but once across the threshold, pushing his way between the broad shoulders of bikers, he had a view of the entire barroom. Emmett, though, would surely have the best view of all.

In the dim light Howdy could see the room was snug, the bar set to one side, a group of wide-backed men mostly standing beside it. A jukebox lit up one corner of the room, the insistence of organ, drums, and Jim Morrison's unmistakable voice pushing past laughter and conversation. At a trio of crowded booths, leather-vested men sat below a haze of smoke, pitchers of beer at the centers of their tables. Beards, muscled arms, heavy black boots. They shouted above the music, calling across the packed room to be served. Howdy tried to edge his way forwards, but several men shoved him to the side. "Hey!" one called in his direction, and heads turned, straightening out this stranger with their stares. Palms sweating, Howdy suddenly formed an unbelievable thirst.

The eyes on him then shifted. A few looked up as Morgan crossed the room, and then it was all eyes on the girl. Howdy recalled the first time he'd seen her, how her walk called for the room's attention. But this time there was a small pig tucked under an arm, his manner interested, his tail tightly curled, and his snout in the air.

More heads turned, and most of those who sat now rose for a better look.

"It's her!" someone yelled, as she pitched the pig lengthwise over the bar, where the bartender, bent over his ice well, stood just in time to see Emmett sail toward him. Suspended for a moment, his legs tucked under his belly, Emmett let out a good, loud squeal before he tipped the Pabst Blue Ribbon handle to full pour and landed none too neatly against the bartender's large belly, knocking him to the floor. Emmett zigzagged past him and managed to make it around the bar to the front door where Howdy gathered him up. The bar filled with shouts and laughter, and soon everyone was buying them shots of whiskey to toast the flying pig.

Emmett stood on the bar and ate a few corn nuts, and the bartender—whose mother, it happened, was Lucille—said Em should come around more often. It was good for business. Men in suede and denim and torn work shirts punched the air, shouting and downing bottles of beer. Howdy noticed there were women here too. A few sat at the bar and flipped their hair back. They touched Emmett's button snout and then squealed themselves. Most of the customers lived in the neighboring town of Silo where much of the state's livestock grain was processed. Funny how things all seemed to come together, thought Howdy.

Still, what puzzled him was the girl. She attracted attention to herself, and yet, she was genuine. She hadn't harmed anyone with her practical joke; it was true. Instead, she'd brought a loud sort of life into his world. To the inquisitive crowd, she gave in and revealed her name and origins, her entire story. "I'm called Morgan, thanks to my Texan father, and Esmeralda, thanks to my Mexican mother," she said. "And Lord only knows about Loving." The youngest of six, the only girl, all five of her brothers shoulder-deep in their father's oil business and their mother's high-society expectations, she recalled the wild boredom of her childhood on the ranch where her mother's peacocks roamed with palominos, where tumbleweeds blew and jackrabbits chased among the mesquite and acacia, the cacti and agave. Then she grew quiet, and the barroom settled, listening in, captured by her tale of travelling north, her direction a near diagonal through Texas and Oklahoma, Kansas and a slip of Illinois, reaching Iowa and its rolling hills, understanding another version of home, her tone gentle and unyielding, assured and pierced with sweetness. She raised her glass, and the bar lights ricocheted from dozens of raised glasses and bottles of beer, and voices called out in celebration of this pig and this girl. Howdy watched Morgan laughing, mostly with the men, and soon realized he was laughing too.

Eventually, the storm came through with pelting rain, and they made their way back to the farm, the little truck thrown around the road by buffeting winds. As they pulled up the drive, funnel clouds flung themselves here and there. Howdy and Morgan pressed through the gale to the house, taking Emmett with them. The electricity had gone out, so they lit candles and Howdy made cold roast beef sandwiches, the crusts of which they gave Emmett along with a few half-eaten apples.

In the wavering light, Morgan stretched and yawned. "I'm so tired," she said. "Aren't you?"

Howdy nodded and led her to the little room that had once been his. She pulled back the red-and-white quilt on the single bed and, fully dressed, climbed under. Her head sank into the old feather pillow, and she closed her eyes. Impressed by how quickly she fell asleep, Howdy watched her for a few moments, then wandered off to his own bedroom, the one that had been his parents', the pig following and settling on the braided rug alongside. He draped his clothes over the footboard, then sat for a second and stared into the darkness. The big bedroom's windows faced east, and soon the sun would rise and wake him.

But it was Morgan who woke him. During the night she slid under the blankets, the old double bed sinking slightly under the new weight. Howdy knew she was there by her warmth and the way she leaned against him, but he didn't say anything, feigning sleep, holding her presence as a sign that things would change. Her hair fell across his shoulders, and he let his hand travel to rest on her arm. He felt her breath on his face and then her mouth against his. Seconds stumbled against each other in his mind until there was no time, only her body—her skin, her arms over her head, removing her blouse, her jeans, the clothes falling to the floor. He looked up at her, then closed his eyes and tried to make sense of his tangled-up desire. But there was no making sense of this feeling—it just was. Morgan loved him right then and there, and he loved her back. She arranged herself, her warm shape around his. Strands of fear, desperation, rapture, and finally an overwhelming calm ran through him. He lay awake and listened to the storm outside, now less riotous, the winds quieting. Emmett slept on the floor nearby, an empty trouser leg draped over his back.

In the morning Morgan was still there. The sun was trying hard to make its way past a layer of thick white clouds, and Morgan was in the kitchen, finding orange juice and pouring it into glasses like she'd always been there. Butter sizzled in a frying pan, and eggs had been broken into a bowl, ready for scrambling. Howdy's mind raced forward to suppers and walks together, fishing out at the back pond, minding themselves and then not minding themselves, gold bands, Emmett's babies, their babies, and the rich smell of breakfast every morning from then on.

"You know, I had a reputation before I came here." Morgan stared at him over her glass. "I grew up in that part of Texas where there's just nothing to do. At night, my brothers and I would steal horses for joyrides, take the doors off our meanest neighbors' work trucks and prop them around their fence lines, then point and lock their weathervanes northeast past Odessa in the direction of Dallas." She set the glass down. "No cows to tip, no pigs to toss. Wrong part of the country. More roughnecks than razorbacks in the high desert." She smiled and then tried not to smile.

"How old are you?" Howdy said, watching her, in love with her new but familiar face.

"Old enough. Why?"

"Can't you answer a question without stalling?"

"Not in my nature." She poured the eggs into the pan and stirred them with a wooden spoon.

"You're young," Howdy said. "But you don't lie."

"My only quality. Gets me into more trouble than lying probably would."

"Okay, now that you're answering questions: What was that we did last night?"

Morgan looked sideways at Howdy. "You don't know?"

"No, no. Oh, no." He hung his head. "I mean earlier, at the bar."

"Nothing fancy. Just had fun. We took a young pig, like this one"—she glanced down at Emmett—"and tossed it in the direction of Lucille's son. A specific direction is always best. Works well if you want to make a point."

"What point exactly?"

The eggs were rising inside the pan, a soft yellow, and there was the scent of bread—biscuits—from the oven. On the kitchen table, plates and silverware were ready. Coffee already poured.

Howdy could see her thinking about the question, and then changed his mind. "Listen, Morgan. I heard you in *Shirley's* last week."

"Now there's a man that could use a pig tossed over his bar," Morgan said, waving the serving spoon.

"Right. Well, I heard what you said about why you'd come here." He sat down at the table. "Well, you've tossed your pig. But who are you and why'd you really come here?"

"There you go again." The words rang out like song.

She crossed the kitchen and served the eggs, fragrant with butter. And as quickly she turned back, opened the oven, and pulled out a sheet of biscuits—high golden biscuits. She loaded a basket with them and returned to the table.

"Sorry, no bacon or sausage. Not a good idea in present company." Emmett sat on the linoleum and grunted. The missing ingredient. Morgan rubbed her bare foot along his back, and he grunted even more loudly.

"Why me?" Howdy asked again.

"Why not?"

"The questions for questions, last night, this morning." He searched Morgan's face and noticed the small mole beside her mouth. "You are unbelievable."

"Why, Howdy, that's the nicest thing anyone's ever said to me." She leaned over and kissed him.

Somehow, he felt she was tricking him, and yet he wished to be tricked. She sat and they ate. When the last remnants of eggs disappeared from their plates, Morgan took Howdy's hand and pulled him out onto the porch. The sun had broken through. A glimmer of light reflected off the pond, and young shoots of grass were coming up in unruly tufts around the yard. The air was warming, though the breeze was still sharp as if coming from a long distance—a cruel distance.

"I want to stay here, with you," Morgan said, staring off into the bare fields.

"I am not sure about all this." He watched her leaning against the porch railing.

Inside, Emmett squealed, and there was the crash of dishes.

Morgan laughed. "You think he wants something?"

"No," Howdy answered. "I think you want something."

"Yes." She approached him. "To stay here."

She touched his cheek, then rested her head on his shoulder. He hardly knew this girl, though he felt he'd known her for some unearthly amount of time.

Howdy's mind filled with odd bits of disorder, and he realized he needed time to think things through. Yet, he'd already spent an entire lifetime doing just that. His father had taught him that life was to be lived carefully. Where had that gotten him? He had to consider the value of a little recklessness in a world that moved too slowly.

Still, he followed the usual weekday schedule until the afternoon when an AG student caught up with him, yelling about a confrontation in long barn # 2. Emmett's former barn. One of the adolescent pigs, a Large White, had gotten loose and was cornering a Tamworth—a young sow who had wandered free of her own pen. Little Lady Tam, thought Howdy. She faced the boar and sniffed the air around him, as if it were perfumed with sweet grain. Almost immediately, the White sat down and stopped his assertive behavior. Howdy instructed the student to lead the male to an outside pen where he could forage, and he took the sow back to her own pen.

Howdy wondered at this uncommon occurrence. There seemed a troublesome absence of logic from his world, a convergence of uncommon events that for some reason he welcomed. He suddenly had the urge to toss something of heft. Something astounding. Something that would call those who knew him to question if they really knew him at all. He lifted the sow from her pen, walked to his truck, and drove home.

At dusk Howdy sat on his porch, Emmett and the unnamed sow in the yard, tearing at heads of cabbage and carrot tops. The sun had long since fallen past the crowns of a westward line of trees and was sinking into the hills and fields beyond. A ruddy pink colored the sky, but the wind stayed constant. In early spring there was always wind. Things blew in: rubbish, torn kites, feathers, battered corn stalks, neighbors' wash from their laundry lines, paper slips from the rough-scented rendering plant down the road.

What had blown into Howdy's life baffled him. He wanted to make sense of it, but then, did it really matter? Morgan's car had run its final mile, and so he had let her take the truck into town. Now that he saw her driving back down the road, a trail of dust rising past the wheel wells and beyond the bed, he was just a little surprised. He hadn't known if she would return, and if she hadn't, he would have gone on as before. But he did know there was nothing she needed; it was what she wanted that struck him. To stay. And so she did.

Weeks and then months passed, and still she stayed. There were walks and meals. There were evenings on the porch colored by the lengthening skies of late spring, the creak of the swing, and the warmth of Morgan's hand inside Howdy's. There was the timbre of her voice, brimming with stories of her family: her Mexican mother of proud lineage, her wayfaring father who carried the beautiful Mexican girl from Chihuahua back to west Texas, the five older roughneck brothers, her arrival as the youngest—the long-awaited daughter—and the dusty plains and tumbleweeds and oilfields that stretched on and on. There was the fact that she and Howdy were sharing the double bed, covered with a new quilt, one lone star in its center. The undercurrent of gossip backed off when Howdy and Morgan married in the Lutheran church in Silo, a circle of Harleys and aged Indian Scouts parked outside. There were piglets underfoot and babies in the making. Howdy was afraid that he would wake up one morning and it would all be gone. He felt like he was standing at the top of the hayloft, looking down on what his life these past thirty years had been. Tools, trampled straw, old tractor parts, the Allis Chalmers manual. One misstep and he'd fall back down there and have to take up his solitary life once more. Somehow he'd managed to stay where he was—in that lofty place—with a wife, a view, and a future. Still, while his life kept on getting more and more real, at times he felt it was undeserved and unreal. Always in the back of his mind, there was the fear that it would all vanish.

When his first child was about to be born, he had to know. He strode out to the barn, took up one of Emmett's piglets and tossed it, ever so gently, into a mound of hay. It landed without injury and trotted off to find its siblings. Howdy felt no inspiration in this—or relief, or amusement, or whatever he should have felt. He felt only dismay. Why, on the day of their first child's birth, would he feel such a thing? The realization was beyond him, and that anything should be beyond him at this point in his life—this inexplicable, upended moment that had become his life—was mystifying. The swirl of emotions pressed in on him, and by the time his son, Clyde, was born—an end to the line of Howards—he was beside himself with dread.

"You look terrible," Morgan said.

He nodded. The bedroom swam before him, the doctor and midwife moving about, and Morgan holding a swaddled newborn.

"Howdy, come sit next to me and see your son." Morgan's maternal beauty blurred into a kaleidoscope of alarming, windswept colors. "Howdy?" The baby she held in her arms was small and pink, like a piglet.

Howdy recalled little of that day. Small cries, friends appearing with casseroles, a bottle of beer that someone seemed to have placed in his hand. Lined with straw and scented with grain, his life blurred before him. That night he fell asleep on the couch and dreamt a dream more real than his waking life, a dream that cut into him, a dream so unadorned, so bare and bewildering, that he couldn't wait to wake up and keep on living. There, inside a sleep as heavy as the air before a cyclone, he dreamt that he tossed his son over a west Texas bar into a line of whisky bottles, the Old Crow shattering as the cloth diaper slid over the glossy wood, before the bartender—who looked nothing like the straight-backed Stran Shirley—caught him in his arms, and everyone in the place applauded.

THAT BITTER SCENT

Still upstate in Tonawanda, working the counter, wearing a pink apron
and a pin with my name printed on it. Evangeline—all spelled out in fancy
letters. Sure is different, Aunt Lillette, than with you and Uncle Auguste in
Terrebonne, but the customers keep me going. The church next door gives us
good business: seven dozen glazed, three dozen crullers, and several boxes of
bear claws every Sunday. And the church ladies keep trying to get me saved,
but I work the double shift on weekends. Funny how that goes.

The photos you sent show there's a lot more oil up in the marsh grass
than anyone's letting on. The church ladies say they're praying for all the fish.
I didn't say, "How 'bout praying for the fisherman while you're at it?"

Give me a holler if the shrimp ever start coming in again. My days here
go one after another, and I'd much rather my white rubber boots to this pink
apron.

I've been thinking about this strange thing that happened a few weeks ago. I
was clearing the counter and staring out the big front window and this bird
came flying straight at the glass. Our regular, Mr. Wiley, he'd been reading
the *Buffalo News*, but then he turned around to see what I was so wide-eyed
about. The sight was something: enormous gray wings, a neck from here to
there, legs tucked up. I just stood there and watched it coming—right at us.
Mr. Wiley raised up off his stool, and news about the oil spill, the World Cup
matches, and Jimmy Dean's last moment on earth all drifted to the floor.

We ran outside, and a few of the ladies coming out the church stopped and crossed themselves. Flight feathers and tufts of down lay scattered around the walkway. The bird had broken its neck. Can you imagine, Aunt Lillette? A heron doing a thing like that?

I remembered when I was just five, running around wild on the shore near Cocodrie where the herons nested. Maman waved her hands at me to quiet down. Like always, she had those pink rosary beads and they caught the sun just right, glinting and shining. I sank into the cool sand by her feet. She had some shadow, you know? She leaned over me and said, "I told you once, chére. Don't let me tell you twice." Even now, Maman still scares me.

It's strange that us Cajuns traveled all that way, from Canada to Louisiana, and now here I am, nearly back where our people came from. Mr. Wiley, who used to be an English teacher, remarked on my name and how Longfellow made it famous. Leaned over his coffee and sweet rolls and asked me if I knew any boys named Gabriel.

I told him, "Sure, I knew Gabe. He was my steady boyfriend." Gave me a funny look, so I said, "It's the honest truth. Nearly got married straight out a high school. Gabe went to work as a rough neck 'cause that's what we do, either fish or work the rigs, and the thought of one more second on his father's fishing boat made him head out. That very first time, though, was his very last. Had a funeral 'stead of a wedding."

By the time I was done talking, the whole place had turned to look at me. Guess I have a way with people, non?

The ladies crowded into the shop this week, every one of them dressed in black. They drank half cups of coffee, and I learned they were waiting to pay their respects at Mr. Wiley's funeral. I felt it, you know? I didn't even know he'd died. I was getting off my shift then and wanted to go along. Somehow I ended up in Mrs. Wiley's limo and sat next to her, holding her hand, still in my uniform. She said I smelled of sweet pastries, which seemed to comfort her.

We drove a little ways and it started to rain. It rained at Gabe's funeral, too. You know, Gabe was a lot smarter than people thought. He read books I haven't even read. Kind of like Mr. Wiley—real smart, but not showing off about it. Mr. Wiley, though, he had a lot more people than Gabe at his funeral.

I thought of the morning Mr. Wiley looked at me over the top of his paper and asked if I'd seen the Falls. I told him no, so he took me across into Canada. Said the Canadians had the best view.

In the park there were tea roses just like at a wedding and honeymoon couples walking the paths. Maybe I should have thought of Gabe and of how Maman passed away so close to our wedding date and just before the rig blew.

But Mr. Wiley, he kept me distracted, talking about poets and their stories and pretty soon there was that view, that wall of water. Bright white and unreal. I had to sit down on a bench and grab hold of the rough wooden slats. Mr. Wiley sat beside me and didn't say anything for a while.

Around us were lantana flowers, yellow and orange, like yours, Aunt Lillette, with that bitter scent of citrus and metal. It was too much. In front of me were those falls, thundering away, but all I could see was the cloudless view of the Gulf from your porch and, up out of the gray-green waters, a thousand seabirds—terns, seagulls, hundreds of brown pelicans—rising into the air. And in amongst the birds I saw Maman in that flowered housedress she always wore, the one with the crab boil stains.

There I was, then, making up my mind to get back home. I'm tired, Lillette. Not as tired as you. I know that. But tired of smelling like sugar and burnt coffee. You know?

GORILLA

In the Berlin Zoologischer Garten, I stare at one gorilla. Her fur is dark, beyond black; her gaze is dark as well, a gaze that moves past shadows into sad, deflated corners. Beside me, my daughter, Alice, kicks at the stray popcorn and leaves, which have blown in through the entry doors. It is March and still very windy. We have come inside the ape house to rest, to be out of the wind for a while.

When Alice, who is four, tires of her kicking game, she stands on tiptoes to peer at Ben, her baby brother, in his carriage. It is one of these fancy Italian buggies with tight navy fabric and enormous wheels. I think about reminding her not to wake him, but then decide not to.

"Mummy?" she says.

"Yes, Alice."

"What do the signs say?"

Above the exhibit are signs, posted in German, and I understand that direct eye contact with the gorillas is ill-advised, *nicht erlaubt, anstrengt verboten*.

I continue to stare at the one gorilla and lie to my daughter, saying, "Oh, those just explain where the animals come from, what they eat, that sort of thing."

Alice nods, almost satisfied. She prances around, then plants her feet and looks at me. "What do they eat?"

I point to the center of the enclosure. In the crook of a dead tree, a young gorilla holds a crescent of yellow melon above his head. He smells the rind.

The female gorilla looks down at the backs of her hands, then turns them over and examines her palms. She appears caught, trapped inside a thought, and covers her face.

I remember arriving home from the dinner party last night, my own hands blocking the sight of him. Peter, my husband, the tall, brooding man that women—strangers—stare at, follow, reach for. Standing in the doorway of our bedroom, still in my coat, I considered walking outside, away from him, from the moment—the unforgiving, relentless disapproval. But I stayed, a fixture in the threshold of a room once lovely and intimate, now cold, its clean lines desperate with angles and perfect order. Perfume bottles of thin hand-blown glass; photographs of the children in sterling frames; an antique hand mirror from the Straße de Siebzehnte Juni Flohmarkt; an invitation to his sister's wedding. All aligned, all placed, as he wished, just so. If ever he found something out of place, he questioned me, repeating my name, Sandra, Sandra—the "S" an accented "Z," brilliant, bare—holding me quickly by the wrist, his grip tightening, twisting if I protested. Had Alice ever heard me cry out?

"Mutti?"

I look down at Alice. She is bored and has begun to speak in German.

"Mutti," she says. "Ich möchte gerne die Flamingo Babies sehen." She reaches inside my unbuttoned coat and pulls at my sweater, at the strap of my camera. "Mutti, bitte," she whines.

I ignore her until she stretches the tweed-colored wool and I feel the yarn start to give.

"Alice, stop that." She leans back, still holding my sweater, her short blond hair flying, full of static. "Alice, stop it right now."

"Nein, ich will nicht!" she shouts.

I lean over the pram. Inside the netting that hangs from the handle are toys, extra blankets, a cloth bag filled with apples the size of Alice's fists. I give my daughter an apple and tell her to stop speaking to me in German. She continues to fuss, but still takes the apple, her rosebud mouth pouting, her bright eyes angry and unkind.

"You know, Alice, you are to speak to me in English," I say. "You know what Daddy wants." I hate what I am saying. If I could just not speak, not say anything at all.

Still, the gorilla covers her face. There is silence now, disturbed only by the thin, reedy sound of wind outside. She is motionless. I wonder if she sleeps. I touch the window that separates us.

* * *

Yesterday, in bed, wrung out by his words, his gestures and posturing, I found myself awake. Peter laced his fingers through my hair. I always gave in—my board of a body, stiff with insult and silent censure, eased and warmed by his touch, by the memory of sex for love's sake. He pulled me close, my thighs in his hands, my lips against his earlobe—breaths, forgetting, a shudder at the center of my spine—uncertainty, even after all these years.

I slept and woke. He was gone. Marissa was in the kitchen with the children, giving them warm rolls and marmalade. Breakfast.

Once we ate in bed, Peter and I. Before the children. Before Marissa—the girl he'd hired to cook and clean and see to the children. For me, he said. So that I had time to myself, he said. But, yes, we'd eaten Brötchen and jam, enormous appetites, the sheets lacquered with spilled fruit and tea, his arms wrapped around me as if the morning had never come. And then we'd walked the boulevard to the Tiergarten: Kurdish children kicking a ball back and forth in the grass, Peter spinning me in circles, the sun falling between the treetops and shattering down around us.

His parents liked me, even though I was American. I suppose my British heritage, all our holidays in Sussex, made up for that. Perhaps it made me seem more European to them. But that was years ago: the days when I interned at Vogue, the long dizzying days amongst the models and photographers, the wide-angle lenses, and the drugs.

Lara was lovely then. Peter's sister, only seventeen. She adored my brown curls, my innocent Stateside demeanor. She was so accepting, so naïve. And I was just three years older. We stole her father's Dunhills and tucked ourselves against their apartment's balcony walls to smoke. An old apartment that had survived the war—its high ceilings laden with ornamental relief, its circular stairways always leading up, vast rooms that through double doors opened even wider revealing leather, parquet, velvet. And the views. The glorious views of the River Spree curving below, while red-tiled roofs cast themselves like roughened kilim beyond the riverbanks. In the street below were voices and sirens, and a scratched jazz record murmured from the open rooms next door. Our backs against the walls, taking in the height, the incredible view, we smoked. Peter joined us sometimes.

Once he asked us how much we cared for him.

"I mean it, really," he said. "How much difference do I make to you two?"

Lara laughed at him. "What are you talking about?" she asked.

I held my cigarette down at my side and watched them lean into each other. Lara grabbed his sleeve and Peter pushed her away—nothing mean in their gestures, just the unfinished sort of touching that brothers and sisters do. I stepped between them, trying to smile, and slowly, still holding the cigarette, divided the air between them with my hand. A thin wall of white smoke, Peter's bright sigh, Lara's arm looped through mine, the impossibility of what might happen.

Lara led me to the balcony's edge, her fingers tightening around mine. She pointed to a child looking out a window across the way. And then she took my face in her warm hands and kissed me. The seconds spun away, and then she laughed—blond and diminutive in the late afternoon light. Peter lingered, a little away from us, and I couldn't quite see him. She did it for my reaction, for Peter's reaction, and afterward—more than anything—I remembered the taste of her, like anise.

Under my hand, the glass begins to fog. The viewing area is completely empty, save Alice tearing at her apple, Ben asleep, and myself. It is almost three in the afternoon. The sun shines at a low angle through the ape house windows, and I become warm, my layers burdensome. Soon Ben will wake and Alice will attempt a bout of jealous fury, the intrepid older sister—how emboldened she is at screaming louder than her brother cries. I will try to calm them and feel hopeless. It is amazing how little I can cope with my children's behavior despite my love for them. For this I bend and surrender my days to Marissa, who is certain and kind and reveals nothing. She is entirely private, without friendship, offering respect only for my position as Alice and Ben's mother.

Earlier, before we left the apartment, Alice chose which camera we should take to the zoo. Peering into the voluminous camera bag and touching the inscriptions of the three cameras, she pulled out the Voightländer and examined it: as always, her curiosity unadorned, almost reckless, but not so much that I felt worried. The small black camera fit in her hands. She held it to her face as if she might take my picture. I guided her fingers to loosen the lens cap, which fell and sat on the hallway runner like a black hole. Alice looked down at it, then kicked it with the rubber toe of her shoe. Then she pointed the camera at me and pressed the shutter release—a slow, metallic sound.

The gorilla uncovers her face. Her eyes are like ocean channels. Like black coral, polished and weighted. She seems tired, and I understand. A sense of the indefinite floats between us: the weight of the afternoon, the heaviness of the indoor air. There are no answers, only demands. Her despondency is measured in the absolute stillness, her gaze searching, her fingers clenched before her unspeaking mouth.

"What do you mean you can't go?" Peter took the tie from around his neck and placed it on his dresser, a long silk line of charcoal.

"I just can't," I said, an undeveloped argument forming at the back of my throat—the glass finials of our bedside lamps reflecting odd, disjointed patterns about the room.

His impatience always grew quickly, an ugly flower. The swift slap, his fingers flying against my cheek, thrust into my clavicle, mostly at my face, where bruises later deepened, dark and violet. I waited for his hand, knowing that I would stay indoors until the marks subsided, covered by layers of foundation, a thick twist of scarves around my neck.

"I don't understand you, Sandra." He seemed to plead, almost beg, and I knew I liked this. This fleeting bit of power. I wanted more: to be in charge, for once; to see his helplessness; to have him love me from the floor, on his knees.

I moved to my bureau, took the invitation, and tore it in two. "I won't go. How much more do you want me to say?" I dropped the white and gold paper at his feet. His shoes were so beautiful, thick Italian leather, almost new.

I expected the back of his hand across my face. Instead, he sat on the edge of our bed, staring at the invitation. The usual blue of his eyes darkened—like night they were. I followed his gaze to the raised letters of Lara's name, the cathedral, the early evening hour, a Sunday wedding. The pale paper lay like ivory, like brittle morning light. Peter's shoulders heaved slightly, and the top of his dark head, appeared soft, approachable. The folds of my coat draped against the bedspread as I sat next to him.

"Lara really plans to go through with this marriage?" I asked. "As if a wedding means a new start? It's all just façade." I glanced at the fine wool of his trousers. "She made promises to us, to me. You know that."

"I don't know anything anymore." His hands rested atop his lap, palms up, one gold band shimmering in the strange light.

I kneeled at his feet and picked up the invitation. His hand grazed my temple. I held the pieces out for him to take, and he did. I lingered, the bare floor hard against my knees as I undid his laces: thin black lines, as thin as his expression when I finally looked up.

Down the hall, Ben began to cry.

"Leave him," Peter said. He pulled me up and grasped me about the waist—gratuitous, reckless movements. I lost my balance and fell into him. I stood there unwillingly, unable to protest, listening to my son wail, while my husband undid the buttons of my coat.

"Mutti, schau mal." Alice laughs. "Look!"

A group of young gorillas chase each other, one of them wielding a long piece of rubber, something like a torn bicycle inner tube. I imagine Ben—who in the past few days has just managed to sit up on his own—as a boy running. He will shriek to his friends just as this gorilla boy calls to his. The tubing flies through the air and hits the window nearest us. Shielding her head, elbows askew, the female gorilla looks at the boys and puckers her lips. She pulls at the tuft of grass where she sits. Verdant, almost too new, the blades between her fingers roll and twist and fall.

In the doorway of the interior house, a silverback stands, his weight forward, easing onto his knuckles. His brow is calm as he surveys the yard. Thick ropes, leafless tree trunks, hillocks, flat expanses lie before him. Here, there is room to move. He swings out onto the grassy surface and spies the female. She ignores him.

Lara has been hospitalized several times. I have tried to give up our friendship. What has become more than friendship, seductive and vague. The clear tubing, that each time cleared the drugs from her thin body, has become an everyday attachment, like so much jewelry. Under stiff white sheets, she would gesture to me with her hands, holding up one finger. One more time, only one more. And I'd think, one more chance, promise, lie. She said she is done with the needles, the late-night lounging in back alleys, in abandoned apartments near the Görlitzer Bahnhof. Her parents, my in-laws, have sequestered her. Only the best facilities, this time on the Baltic coast, a place where everyone is a stranger, where the wind is strong and clean. Just like she will be, strong and clean. Of course, she will. In time for the wedding.

Who is this man she is marrying? A filmmaker? A man who will give her every freedom. I wonder if he will beat her. If he would limit his blows to the midriff, the area right above the kidneys, never approaching her face except to caress it gently. Or perhaps a lawyer? Able to treat her fairly, justly, handcuffs safe in the bedside drawers, secrets under her long sleeves. Surely not an architect—like Peter. Elegant, fine house of a man. Everything in straight, clean lines. Expectant, amused, preferring a fine wine to an old Scotch. When the unexpected throws him off, he is embarrassed. To answer for his embarrassment is often painful.

Last night I looked at myself in the bathroom mirror, past the flanking sconces illuminating my face and throwing shadows over my shoulders. My throat was scarlet from Peter's trimmed beard, from the stranglehold meant to quiet me while our baby screamed in the background. Once, I found him stunning, exquisite, unequaled. No, I still did. I knew there was no such thing as redemption. He affirmed his displeasure—of my latest photographs, of my afternoon absences, of my friendships with people he didn't know—and I embraced the brutality. Without it, there was no breath, only despair. I had my children, my lovely children. And so I held on—to the bedpost, to the towel rack, to anything that might hold me beneath the beautiful weight; a weight so unforgiving and yet, strangely, unfathomably desirable.

* * *

The female gorilla approaches the window. Her head is angled. Does she see me, or her own reflection? Slowly, she places her hand on the glass. I move mine so that it is even with hers. Cautious, I look sideways at the pram, at Alice who sits on a bench now, staring at her fallen apple, moving it gently with the toe of her small blue shoe. Looking back at the gorilla, I see her eyes widen with an immediacy that is startling. She must see me.

Lara's eyes are dark and layered with colors like green and gold. When I was pregnant with Alice, Lara told me that her father beat her. The first time, when she turned seventeen, the night of her birthday. Delirious with champagne and in love with a boy named Kai, she scarcely remembered her father shouting and crowding her. Later, when her mother was away in Schleswig-Holstein, caring for her dying grandmother, he reproached Lara and her love of sullen boys, comparing his disappointment of her with his anger. And then, whenever he could. Passing through the hall, a simple slap for her bad marks in school; his hand against her shoulder, crushing her, telling her to be good; in the kitchen, before her mother, his wife, a whispered good morning, a threat.

I tried to understand and found myself not understanding at all.

"How can a father beat his daughter?" I asked her.

"You don't know?" she said. "Really?"

We stood in my kitchen on a winter afternoon. Marissa had put bread in the oven, and its sweet aroma cut into the day like too much disagreement.

"He was jealous," Lara said. "He never knew how to talk to me. He liked damage more than words. He could get more results that way."

"Jealous?" I leaned against the closed window. In the courtyard the sound of heels—someone leaving the building—echoed upwards. "That's a reason?"

She shrugged her shoulders. Her response felt its way into the room, evasive and numb.

"Did you ever tell Peter?" I asked.

In the kitchen, surrounded by the smell of baking bread, she laughed at me. Later, I laughed at my own stupidity. We wives and daughters lean into the strength of our men; we are meant to be hit, to be struck, to be rendered into so much senseless beauty.

"Mummy?" says Alice. She stands next to me, looking up at the female gorilla and me, our palms separated only by a window.

"Nicht jetzt," I say.

"But I still want to see the flamingo babies," she says. "You promised."

"We'll go in a moment," I say, my voice shaking, my hand still on the glass.

In a swirl of gray and black, swift and massive, an enormous explosion of movement and sound, the silverback rushes the window. He flies at us—large, unburdened, unbelievable. I am convinced he will kill the female and then crash through the window and maul us. Alice grabs my sweater, this time curling her fingers through the wool, and buries her face in the weave of my coat. Children believe that by hiding, by not looking, anything frightening will go away. I am glad that Alice still has this to hold onto. For me, there is no reason to look away. I remain there, hand against the glass. Immovable.

The silverback is enraged. He strikes out once, at air. The female continues to hold her padded black palm against the glass. Her great nostrils widen, and she pushes against the window, the tips of her leathery fingers almost touching mine, dwarfing my smaller, paler hand. I am amazed at the silence of her stance, the dignity. Alice begins to cry.

Inside of her small cry is the guilt and fear that I know all too well—the times she certainly has witnessed her parents at odds, late at night, when she should be sleeping. Muffled breaths and blows, the open bedroom door. And eventually night becomes day, and in the daylight we go along: we are a quiet family. Peter has never shouted at me. But Alice knows. Her father has always been quiet. Controlling and exacting and so very sure—his blows measured to the millimeter.

The silverback roars and bares his teeth—yellow and wicked, covered with strands of saliva. He is so close. His face is furrowed with dark, weathered lines extending from his enraged eyes. His breath is heavy, and there is a thick odor, which marks the afternoon like a mistake. Alice glances out from the folds of my coat and screams, the immense gorilla above her, on the other side of the double-thick glass, bellowing and beating himself. I am unfastened by my daughter's terror, her tumultuous emotion, by the unbearable din. The viewing area reverberates with loud, horrific sounds; still, I hear Ben's slow, small cries.

The female gorilla stands at the window, not moving. Her eyes deepen and then glaze over. She blinks, a quiet comment on the unavailability of deliverance. Not today, not tomorrow. The silverback strikes against the window near her head. The crack of his knuckles against the glass is quick, and the quickness of the sound is undone only by the female's expression, not one of surprise, but of expectancy. I am outside of myself, beating on the glass, shouting, not shouting.

Peter caught my arms before I could cut myself on the shattered mirror. In the web of reflection, I watched as he pulled me down to the floor. Again, the bathroom—the tiles hard and grooved but never cold, a layer of hot water pipes snaking beneath.

"Sandra," he said. "How could you have done this to yourself? Tell me that you won't hurt yourself again."

I lay beneath him and listened to the concern in his voice—his mouth close to my ear and his breath unlocked; his legs over mine; his hands tangled in my hair, surrounding the crown of my head—to the idea that this should be so obvious, that this sort of passion was granted to him and him alone. My betrothal to him, his allegiance to me—a sweaty, despicable thing—our marriage. The sex, sweet and brutal, and then the abandonment, how he left me there on the floor.

In the morning Marissa found me, my nightgown swaddled against my legs. She never asked, only helped me find a towel, a fresh soap, a cup of linden tea.

Lara understood. That is why she told me long ago of her father's attempts to silence her. That is how she knew to bring me tranquilizers. We lay in my bed together that afternoon when Peter was at work and Marissa out with the children, shopping. And then on another afternoon, our palms together, promising. She studied me, then kissed my hands and my face again and again. She lied to me about love, telling me that it was more suited to those who could keep quiet. She didn't know if I was capable of that kind of silence. She emptied the bottle into my open hand. More pills and more promises.

The pink of her face, the cant of it. She seemed as insubstantial as a photograph. The dark and the light of it; the shame and the dare of it.

"It all started because of you," Lara said. "You are too beautiful and too talented." She tucked a stray strand of hair behind my ear. "And too intelligent."

"What?" My thoughts had already blurred against the neat white pill, the second, the third, the long swallow of water that Lara had given me.

"The men in our family." For some reason she smiled and then stroked my arm. "They don't like that in women. It's too dangerous, or something."

The familial secrets, the bedroom whispers. Lara unwrapped promises like they were meaningless. She attempted tenderness, but I recognized only cruelty in her tone. It is one thing to make a promise and another to keep it close. Peter had known all along about his father and Lara and then about Lara and me. What began by his own introduction—that kiss on the balcony— had become more than love between sisters. And still, I remained with him, acquiescent. I gave into the durability of his anger. Lara would marry and perhaps know the same. She'd let go of what we'd had. The promise fell, frail but not quite forgotten, at the edge of our friendship. Wide boulevards, innumerable beatings. Still, the family name linked us.

* * *

The gorilla house becomes hushed. Alice tugs hard at my sweater, the hem, the sleeve. Ben whimpers, his moment for attention muffled under quilted layers. Silence presses us all into submission. The silverback watches from the highest vantage point, pacing. The female gorilla has turned her back to me. She appears to sigh, and I believe she is waiting. For more room, for a lost breeze, for a different view. She tilts her head back as if to look up. I imagine her eyes are closed; I imagine the jungle of her mind, crowded with thick green vines, with fragrant lush trees, with hope of reaching out and brushing the brilliant clouds beyond.

THE LAST I SAW MITSOU

The last time I saw Mitsou, she was crying into an embroidered handkerchief that belonged to my mother. Mother believed in things that lasted. Linen, perfume, clothbound books.

Newlyweds, Mitsou and I lived in the fifth-floor walkup. Small rooms with enormous views. Below us, the courtyard, mottled with pale brown stones. Our windows faced the pianist, swaying over his black-and-ivory keys; the small child, her mouth wide for more porridge; and the old man, alone except for a stuttering television.

Three months into our marriage, the books appeared in corners of the courtyard. Poetry in the flowerpots, nursery rhymes tucked under drainpipes, thin historical volumes near the ash cans. Mitsou proposed they had been left there for a reason. She turned their pages, sighing, and placed them gently back into their niches and nooks. Wistful, she recalled her father's print shop, the tinny odor of ink, the shudder of the presses. Her childhood was spare, while mine was ample. She had only her father; I had mostly my mother. I wanted to ask about the illustrated cookbooks she'd found after he'd disappeared, but I couldn't find the words.

Soon after, the novels appeared. Malraux, Genet, Zola. Flaubert, Proust, Voltaire. Stacked like bricks in the courtyard entrance, preventing passage so that we had to use the main doors. Coming and going lost meaning, defined now by the dark hallway lined with mailboxes that no longer received letters, only literary reviews.

Mother called. "The wedding, the wedding, the wedding," she shouted in her typical triplicate. "So glorious, glorious, glorious!"

Mitsou nodded, as I held the receiver away from my ear.

"I'm coming by train, train, train. Thursday next, at seize heures!"

"We'll be there to meet you," I promised.

"You'll be there," Mitsou said. "I'll be here, preparing the trout for dinner. Meunière or Amandine?"

Thursday came. Mitsou set down the platter of sautéed trout, golden, scattered with splintered almonds.

"Lovely fish, fish, fish!" my mother said.

"Merci," Mitsou replied.

Mother had brought presents. "Things you might need, need, need." Repoussé butter knives, damask napkins. "You certainly don't need anything to read, read, read." Her voice flew out the open windows.

The courtyard filled with evening sounds. The child, having her bath and singing sweetly. The old man, watching Jean-Paul Belmondo films, a tall bottle of beer beside him. The pianist, leaning over Chopin's Prelude, Opus 28, # 4 in E minor.

Mother and Mitsou stood at the window, whispering of fathers, fish, and faraway things. "So strange, strange, strange," Mother said, pointing to the book-studded doorway.

Early next morning Mother opened a transom in the crowded passageway. She'd extracted *Germinal*, a rough red *Candide*, *Madame Bovary*—moth-eaten, unbound—and a tattered *Time Regained*.

"It's very sad, sad, sad!" she cried up to our window. "Where, where, where are the cookery books?"

Weeping, Mitsou ran downstairs to Mother, who handed her the kerchief from inside her sleeve. Mother pointed to the gap, narrow and bright, and that was the last I saw my Mitsou, climbing through to the other side.

IN THE GREAT WIDE

On a warm day in May, some years ago, Mary's uncle set up a crawfish boil for his family of twenty-five and ended up feeding the five hundred members of St. John's Cathedral. Hard red crawdad shells piled up on the newspaper-covered picnic tables, and the altar boys swore the ice-cold beer never ran out. Across town that same spring, in the churchyard where my parents' graves had already shifted in the soft soil, swarms of cream-colored roses grew, though no one had planted them. In late summer, a hurricane's eye rested over the delta while the outer storm stalled and eventually gave up. The winds changed to light breezes, and the sideways rain became a calm, sighing mist. That autumn a rumor floated through the neighborhood that the dying old woman one street over had woken up twenty years younger. By evening she was an infant in her daughter's arms, and before the moon rose, she had disappeared.

And then there was the Saturday afternoon I came home with my friend Mary from the winter sales down on Canal Street. We were breathless from walking all those blocks from the streetcar stop, the day's gray cast and our thin-handled shopping bags weighing us down. As we neared the corner, a bloom caught in a crack in the sidewalk made us both pause. A fist of tiny white roses reached up, the same kind we had read of in Catechism class, the ones associated with Ste. Thérèse of France. Mary crossed herself and whispered, "Another miracle." We didn't even think of plucking them from the crevice and walked on. Miracles kept crowding in, taking up space.

I preferred to think of my own miracle, baby Daphne, nearly a year old, growing in a new way. In the weeks since Mary's last visit, Daphne had changed so much that I wondered how Mary would take to seeing her.

The little house on Prytania Street where I lived with Maman Yvette and Daphne seemed to lean out as we crossed the front steps to the covered porch. The cat was there, with its amber eyes and missing whiskers, its crooked tail swishing. Mary called the cat a disgrace, but it was nothing less than ugly and affectionate. I placed the key in the lock and pushed the door open with the big bags from the Maison Blanche, blocking Mary's view. I stepped inside, just past the threshold, and stopped. There was Maman Yvette sweeping the hall floor, the baby, just a sweet round head now, rolling around at her feet. My grandmother held the broom still, and the baby swiveled in place like a top coming to rest after a long spin.

I inhaled, hoping what I was seeing was not so. And yet I knew it was. Maman seemed to take no notice, so perhaps I was just imagining the logical next step to the slow disappearance of my baby. Rather than react, I wouldn't show Mary how surprised or shocked or even afraid I truly was. Instead, I'd be mature. I'd be calm. I'd show her I could handle these sorts of things.

"Maman," I said. "What is Daphne doing out here? Shouldn't she be napping?"

Daphne smiled and cooed, her round cheeks pink from play. Blond wisps of hair stood up from the top of her head, messy with the dust from Maman's pile.

Much shorter and more impatient than me, Mary pushed me forward, the cat chasing past us, its tail up. Maman stood to one side and motioned for us to come in.

"What you doing in the door? Move on through, chères." She pulled on Mary's sweater and said, "May-ree, how is your mother?"

"Why, she's all right, Maman Yvette." She patted my grandmother's shoulder, all the while moving down the hall. "She's got the lumbago like she gets sometimes, but she's okay."

Mary looked around me and my shopping bags and started to wave at Daphne, and then stopped with her hand still held in midair. I guess she expected to see all of my eleven-month-old because she pushed me aside and said, "What? Qu'est-ce qu'elle a?"

She tiptoed past Daphne and the dust pile, her hands at her mouth, her eyes fixed. I could tell by her hard, questioning stare that she'd never seen a bodiless baby before. And Daphne hadn't always been this way. In fact, I was just getting used to it myself.

On Monday, my baby's melon head had looked more prominent than usual, while her belly, bottom, thighs, and chubby little arms had begun to diminish. But when I gave her a cup to drink from, she held it just fine. I set her down on the carpet and she crawled and cruised the sofa, reaching for her rattle and shaking it at the cat. By Wednesday, her body had begun to fade, her face to brighten; she seemed content to sit in her highchair, watching the cat clean herself or Maman pan-fry croaker fish. This morning before I left to catch the streetcar, Daphne slept. Her flannel covers felt lighter, as if covering more of a thought than a body. Still, my baby girl looked peaceful, her breaths slow, her small rose mouth open. I realized later that she hadn't been sucking her thumb. Now it made sense.

I put down my bags and reached for Daphne. She laughed and rolled across the black-and-white tiles away from me. She reminded me of the bright child-sized bowling balls at Trinity Lanes: how they crashed along, then wobbled against a few pins, and finally zoomed back in line with the darker adult-sized balls to wait for another turn. Mary, in charge of the Orleans Parish leagues down at Trinity, probably wouldn't have appreciated my association. At the end of the hall, she made a long shadow, her lean body blocking the window, her hands on her hips.

"Antoinette? What in the world?" Mary had a pretty set of eyes. Green-hazel against her light brown skin. At that moment they slanted, like half-closed doors.

"You mean Daphne?" I knew exactly what she meant. "She's fine. Just fine."

"I beg your pardon, but your baby has no body." Mary's eyes narrowed, and she pointed at Daphne. "There is nothing fine there. What can you possibly mean by fine?"

"Oh," I hesitated. "I know it looks strange and all. But in the great wide scheme of things, we really are quite all right."

"Quit standing in my hallway. I'm trying to work here." Maman shooed us down toward the kitchen, while Daphne disappeared into the sitting room.

"Great wide what?" said Mary. "Have you all lost your minds? Daphne is rolling around the house like a bouncy ball, and y'all are all right with this?"

I glanced away from her toward the sitting room and my bags. The diapers I'd bought would no longer be needed. Nor the new playsuits and frilly dresses. I felt like I'd lose my mind, but not in front of my friend.

"You know me, Mary," I said, trying hard to push away the sense of dread that was climbing inside me. "I always try to look on the bright side of life. Just think, Daph will never have to worry about her body image."

"You are too crazy, Antoinette." Mary looked off down the hall, distressed, and then started to cry. "Too, too crazy for me. What are you going to tell all your cousins? And our friends? How will Daphne be able to play and learn and later on have a family of her own? You haven't thought of that, now, have you?"

"Oh, Mary." I sat on the edge of the kitchen table, suddenly exhausted by my own lies. "It's all so new. We'll figure it out as we go along. I know it will be all right, and we are sure to find the rest of her."

"You are too at ease. Have you called the doctor or the priest? The Mother Superior?" She took my chin in her hand, gently at first, and then cuffed me a bit. "Your child's almost nonexistent, and you're sitting there. What will you do if she vanishes altogether? Have you thought about that?"

"I told you," I said and pushed her hand away. "It's all new. We're just getting accustomed to these changes." I crossed my arms, the prickly sweep of panic rising through my mind. "That all right with you, Miss Mary? If it's not, then you'd best be on your way."

Winter sun streamed around my friend, her silhouette engraved into the surrounding light. Dark curls fell against her face, and a cool breeze from the open window lifted them. From the courtyard, a lone mockingbird called, in the beginning melodious, then with a chirring, rattling note. Mary gazed at her own feet, then at me. The saddest look ever.

"What will you do?" she said, wiping away her tears. And then her gaze widened. "Why, those little sidewalk roses have told us already. You should pray to Ste. Thérèse of Lisieux. You remember Ste. Thérèse?"

Mary called up saints out of desperation. We lapsed Catholics knew they were there, abundant, just waiting for us to utter their names. I remembered Ste. Thérèse, "the Little Flower," that nineteenth-century child whose mother died when she needed her most. She was only ten years old and prayed to Our Lady. For what, though? Divine inspiration? For Our Lady to take up the call as a stand-in mother? I knew these prayers all too well. Ever since the summer my parents died, drowned in the Gulf, their bodies never found in the hurricane wreckage. Despite our grief, the Catholic Church had looked down on Maman and me. Ours was a piteous solo state, without the strength and guidance of men, and later with our bastard baby.

For me, divine inspiration wasn't found in a communion wafer, or with a boy named Val in the back seat of a Chrysler, but only in the sweet, fragile breath Daphne took between sleeping and waking. Body of Christ, body of the boy who fathered Daphne, body of the babe gone before our eyes. Was this then a punishment for my sins? While Maman said her rosary and went to Mass every day, I was completely remiss, purposely avoiding prayers, certain that no saint would ever help us.

And yet, if Daphne did fade away, no longer a baby, but a memory, what would I do? Since her birth, life had become glad and loud. All the neighbor ladies had called out to the laughing baby when I'd sat with Daphne on the porch steps during the slow summer and fall evenings. Maman had taken to pushing the stroller around the block several times a day, so proud she was of her great-granddaughter. And down at the bowling lanes, Mary had shown off Daphne and even said she'd brought good luck to her game.

Before Daphne, there had been a half-light to the world, a half-meaning to words, half a reason to wake up most mornings. Would we return to all of that? Would the vibrancy die away or echo into the empty rooms if my baby disappeared? Would St. Anthony roam our house calling out for her little lost soul? I refused to consider that fool saint; after all, my baby girl wasn't missing; no, indeed not. She was just quieter.

I thought of the time when Daphne had started crawling. Bright with her newfound motion, she had banged and called and scooted around the house. Slapping her high-chair tray for more, more, more. Waving at the cat, at Maman, at me. But she was still here; she hadn't gone off into thin air. I looked at Mary now. I was not going to spend time lingering over what might be. My baby was still living and breathing in this very house.

"Maman," I called. "Would you fix Mary some tea? She looks about to faint."

Maman shuffled into the kitchen and set her broom in the corner. "I'll make you some good chamomile. Come on, May-ree. Sit down."

I guided my friend into a kitchenette chair and smoothed down her hair. "St. Thérèse was all about staying calm and untroubled. In the Lord's hands and all," I told her.

"We got them cookies from down by Meraux's Bakery, too," said Maman. "You take some a those to your mama, May-ree. For while she's resting up. C'est bien, n'est-ce pas?"

"That's right, Maman," I said. "You take care of Mary. I'm going to get the baby."

Daphne was asleep under Maman's sewing table, and tenderly, I picked her up and carried her to our bedroom. The small sphere of her head, so much lighter than her whole being, surprised me. Its weightlessness beguiled and startled me all at the same time, feelings that pushed against each other and called me to notice, rather than react. There was a small bruise above her left eye, and her lips seemed pale. Easing her gently, my hands cupping her ears, I settled her into her crib. Her downy head tilted back against the pillow, and its small weight made an impression in the eiderdown. I drew up the white flannel blanket fringing her chin and cheek.

I recalled the Valentine's Day when Mary and I were eleven, the first time in years it had snowed in New Orleans. Traffic snarled around the city, but the streetcars kept running. Mary and I gathered a bucketful of snow, and on top of Maman's old Chrysler we fashioned a small but fat snowman, more head than body. When we went to bed, our snowman was still sitting on the hood of the car, but by eight o'clock the next morning the sun was strong enough to melt most of the snow. Once we finally woke up, the snowman was gone. Not even a puddle remained, just a flat shine of dirty water against the dented hood.

I wouldn't admit it to Mary, but I was afraid. Afraid I would blink and Daphne would be gone, a flat shine of memory where once a sighing, laughing life had been. Daphne was my one success in life. My success breathed in and out—her sleep secured her into place.

In the kitchen Mary stared into her tea. She barely glanced up as Maman wiped the counter and nudged the cat with her foot. Dressed in a cotton shift, Maman did what she always did—kept house. She minded us children, whatever generation, whether family or friends, cooked her country-French meals, swept up, sewed, and tended a backyard garden. She preferred babies over solitude, and solitude over men, so it never surprised me when she sang love songs, rather than lullabies, to Daphne. She sang in French, the notes high and wavering, winding through the rooms of the house and resting in the alcoves. The songs warned of heartbreak and despair, never happiness, but Daphne always fell into peaceful, smiling slumbers before they even ended.

Now Maman hummed to herself, setting the teakettle back on the stove, then lit into a line of song, and just as quickly stopped. She sighed and smiled at us. Small, curling violets accented her apron, and she held her damp hands against the fabric to dry them.

"I'm going to lie down, chères," she told us. "All this day I'm so tired."

As she passed, she patted my arm. We were good to each other, no matter what.

"That's right, Maman," I said. "You go on then."

I heard her lie down in her bedroom, a short ways down the hall, the old box springs creaking as she settled herself.

Mary looked over at me, her brow still creased and worried. "Do you remember that time when we were little, and we weren't allowed to go out?" she said. "All that rain."

"Yes," I said, sitting down across from her. "Why?"

"I was just thinking about how it will all be different for Daphne."

In that warm, humid spring of 1967, it rained and rained. Water rose to the top step of the front porch. Mary and I were seven, and the days rushed toward our first Holy Communion. Our white dresses hung in our rooms, the dried flower wreaths for our hair, the silk sashes that, we were told, had turned from shining white to pale ecru over the years since our mothers had worn them for their first communions.

Impatient with the long days, not allowed to traipse farther than that top step, our mothers' collective fear of snakes and other vermin washing up out of the sewers kept us pinned in place. And so we sat barelegged on the porch floor making paper sailboats. We lined them up, then sent the entire fleet out into the floodwaters. Construction paper sails of red, blue, and gold waved from the crimped lids of our tiny milk-carton vessels. Most of them sank, but some made it all the way to the tops of the drowned azalea bushes before tipping.

Mary, whose uncle had a sailboat he kept moored out on Lake Pontchartrain, called out orders. "Set the sails, shift to starboard, hoist the jib, weigh the anchor!"

"All right already," I said. "Don't be so bossy."

"Somebody has to be the captain. What with seventeen ships in heavy seas and the wind at forty knots!" Mary put her hands on her hips. "Do you want to play or not?"

No, not really." I glanced at our tipped vessels. "All the boats are sinking."

Out in the street, water reached halfway up parked cars, door handles just above the water line. An old man paddled by in a flat-bottomed boat. He wore a light blue shirt with the sleeves rolled up to his elbows, and a thin white beard covered his face. As he rowed past, the smell of fish traveled toward us with the wind. He paused a moment to look up, to survey the windows above our heads as if to make sure everything was secure, then seeming satisfied, he nodded and stroked quietly through the murky water.

Mary stared after him. "It's St. Andrew himself," she whispered. "He's laid down his fishing nets and come to bless our fleet." She motioned to the paper boats, all upright in the slight wake of the apostle's pirogue.

Now in the kitchen, Mary took my hand and squeezed. "Daphne needs us now. She needs us to make this right." She looked hard at me then. "What could you have done to deserve this, Antoinette?"

I tried to pull my hand away, but she held on tight.

"There must be a reason for this," she said. "What did you do?"

"What are you saying?"

"This must be some sort of punishment, but maybe if you atone, just seek out some sort of forgiveness…" And then she let go of my hand. "You haven't even prayed yet, have you? Oh, no, you haven't even prayed. I can tell by the look on your face."

I shook my head. "You know I don't pray. There's no sense in it anymore."

"Oh, I think there is. I think there is now." She stood up and nearly tipped her chair over. "I'm going straight over to St. John's. If you won't pray, at least I can petition a saint or two. Somebody out there is bound to hear." She walked to the back door and slowly turned the knob. "St. Anthony, sir, take a look around. Something is lost and must be found." Her voice was loud and cross. Next she'd be calling out to St. Jude, the saint of lost causes.

The back door shuddered open and shut, and I watched her cross the courtyard, the cat close behind her. I'd never felt astonishment, the kind that had taken hold of Mary those years ago on the afternoon of the flood. She was carried away all that spring by silent prayers, the perfumed trails of incense, the shadowed confessional, the polished circle of rosary beads. St. Andrew this and Ste. Brigid that. Patrick, Francis, Valentine. A sanctified slew of saints.

But after a while she came to her senses, threw her palm against her forehead, and traded in novenas and Mass for bowling. These days she had both the church and the lanes to guard her spirit. From her devout period, though, I held fast to Ste. Brigid. All children born out of wedlock and into the church's gridlock needed Brigid. She watched over babies like Daphne and mothers like me. Babies without fathers, young mothers without husbands.

I considered all that I'd done in eighteen years. Too much. Not enough. Maybe Mary was right somehow. All the times I'd left through that same back door. Maybe I'd done it all wrong.

He came from a Garden District family. Tall, blond, curious, romantic, and a year older. Charles Valmont was his name. Val.

My parochial school and his private boys' academy bordered each other, like so much of New Orleans, thrown together despite differences. Almost every night we met in the Irish Channel. Maman never asked why I wanted to borrow the Chrysler. She simply waved to me as I left each evening. "You done your homework, chère?" she asked, and I answered, "Oui, Maman," then waved in return. And Mary? Mary was absorbed in her new spiritual life, every waking hour at the Trinity Lanes, bowling her way past the sacraments. She worked on her form, joined a league, and no longer worried about God's grace. There were no questions about where I went; I was free to do as I pleased.

I parked outside the Half Moon, a bar that welcomed anyone who could pay. Before I even had the driver's door closed, Val was at my side, his arm around my waist. We ate oysters and drank from sweating bottles of beer, then drove to the end of Canal Street to catch the ferry across the river to Algiers, to look out on the city lights, their image broken by the Mississippi's current. And later, all too impatient, we parked outside the Lafayette Cemetery, a midway point between our homes. On the quieter Coliseum Street side, under the shadow of crepe myrtles, we leaned into each other night after night. Large pink blossoms fell onto the windshield and covered the glass in soft clusters, the patter of their green husks startling us at times. One evening we stole into the cemetery, and Val showed me his family's burial vault, its stone corners crumbling, the whitewashed stucco embellished with vines and inscriptions, the name VALMONT curving above our heads.

By summer he had graduated from the academy. His departure for Europe was prefaced with farewells, his face flushed and damp with tears, but I never heard from him again. I imagined that he quickly forgot me. That he went on to college, a decent southern university, to study philosophy or history and court young ladies more suited to his standing in life. From across a room, how would he see me now? My hair pulled back, not loose around my shoulders, and the shadows under my eyes turned darker. And he, searching the room for someone he knew, blinking, not finding me. Sometimes I supposed him already dead among his ancestors in that cemetery vault.

I dropped out of school halfway through my senior year to have the baby. Daphne looked just like her father—not that he would ever know. And I never told anyone who he was. Not even Mary. Maman said the saints would preserve us, just like they always did. I took a job at a nearby variety store, working the counter and keeping the books. Maman seemed happy that I'd grown up, that we always had just what we needed, not more, not less.

Outside the kitchen window, past the scroll of security bars, the courtyard looked quiet. Lines of mossy bricks and banana trees cast the idea of green into corners and up walls. Even in winter New Orleans kept a slow breath of summer in its gardens: even with a chill in the air the soil could still hold warmth, and a hard freeze could undo water pipes but not camellias in bloom. Daphne had been born on a February afternoon, almost one year ago during Carnival, a bundle in the hand-crocheted blanket that Maman had finished just in time. On leaving the hospital, we'd made our way slowly, the buses and streetcars held up at intersections throughout the city until the parades had passed by. Daphne had cried only once.

The girl in my life who cried all the time was Mary. And when she cried, she was downright hysterical. There was no such thing as kind weeping with Mary. Oh, no. She bawled and wrung her hands and worried her handkerchief and on and on. Countless occasions. When the snowman melted. When she missed being the Virgin Mary in the Nativity play because of the measles, and then, the following Christmas when Sister Alphonse chose another girl to play the part. When those girls from the Jeff Parish bowling league greased up Mary's ball with Crisco right before a tournament. When her longtime beau Cecil Thibault asked Alice Parker to the prom. When her husband, Augustus, left. And when he came back. And, of course, long ago when my parents died. Mary was just high-strung and emotional. But gorgeous girls can get away with tears.

I didn't cry much myself. I had no time for tears and nonsense. I had responsibilities. Besides, Mary cried enough for the both of us.

I closed the window. The afternoon had grown cold, and the daylight gave way to the dim edge of evening. Potatoes and onions lay scattered by the sink. Usually, Maman had prepared supper by now. I was too tired myself to take up washing and peeling them.

I walked into the sitting room and crouched at the tiled fireplace. With a long-handled match, I lit the gas burners. The ceramic coils brightened, glowing copper and orange, and the sweet smell of gas grew faint as I opened the valve. The flame spread in a wave of colors. Gold-rust-blue. I held my hands closer, trying to summon that spring: the warmth of the weather, of laughter, of kissing. With Val, sweet-tempered, sometimes drunk, always searching my stare for something mysterious. Spring meant rain and floods and fooling around in the backseat of the old Chrysler and come July the slightest bulge of a belly.

"Don't even try getting into that new dress or that fitted one-piece, girl," Mary had said. "You are going to be sitting right here all summer long." From her spot next to me on the steps of the Prytania Street house, she looked over at the parked cars, the passing traffic, then back at me. She blinked, her eyelids weighted. "And you can kiss the damned poolside good-bye."

Maman peered from the attic window. "May-ree, you had better watch your young mouth, nah." She shook her finger. "You all gonna stay on that stoop the rest of your lives if you don't behave." Then she waved a small rug, and the dust fell over us.

"She has no idea?" Mary asked. She lifted the long, heavy curls off her neck and piled them on top of her head, as she waited for an answer.

"Of course, she knows," I said. "She's up there right now looking for my old baby clothes. Had me up there earlier, searching out the crib. The one I slept in myself, and my mother before me." I paused. "Maman knows everything. But what can she say? She did the same thing herself. My mother was born when Maman was sixteen." Another long, warm day upon us, I pressed my restless hands into my lap, trying to still them. "My mother was more sensible. She waited for marriage and followed the rules. It's a wonder I ever got here."

"Only the Lord knows about that," said Mary.

"Yeah, right," I said. "The Lord knows a whole lot about us Catholic girls. What we need is a miracle."

Mary laughed. "You gonna get a miracle all right. In about six more months, you're going to have a real live little miracle."

I stood up from the hearth and peered into the adjoining room. Evening light silvered the walls above Daphne's crib. My daughter was awake, and her bright murmuring called to me. Movement, a tangle of white blanket, feet kicking the air, dimpled hands reaching up. I gazed down at my baby. She held the ear of a tiny blue lamb, a gift from Mary.

"Look at you."

I held onto the crib's railing. She was there, all there, as if nothing had happened. As if nothing unfamiliar and frightening had ever passed us by. I held onto her presence and barely breathed. Daphne's tiny feet and fat little arms searched the air for me, her mama. The silence and the darkening day seemed to swallow the moment, and I felt startled by its mystery. Just then, the cat leaned into my ankles, and I felt her tail flick the hem of my skirt. I looked down to see a swirl of calico moving back and forth.

"How did you get back inside?"

She purred, reached up with one paw, and caught her claws in my skirt. I leaned over to whisk her away and, when I stood back up, Daphne was gone. I stayed still for a second, thinking the dim light was deceiving me, but then tossed back the blanket and ran my hands over the smooth cotton sheets. There was a warmth to them, as though someone had just slept there, the memory of a small body still evident in the crinkled white cloth. Where her face would have been, should have been, there was dampness, as if she had drooled during her nap.

Until now, I had felt a strange calmness, like a hand at my back, large and reassuring. The calm ruptured and a hot shameful fear overcame me. This was the fear of desperation and panic and disorder. It had been there all along.

I tore the sheets apart and pulled at the edges of the mattress until it landed sideways. I looked under the crib, in the closet, behind the curtains. Everywhere. And then I thought I glimpsed a slight shift in the room. The rocking chair swung forward, then back.

"Daphne?" My voice crawled back inside my mouth.

The cat meowed loudly.

I ran from the bedroom into the hall, the cat underfoot. She chased after me, and I nearly fell into the little telephone alcove. There, a table, a straight-back chair, the heavy black phone, the slim gold pencil and small white pad, and Maman's ancient address book all awaited the next call. I opened the address book and searched for the pediatrician's number. But it was too late for that: Daphne was gone. I flipped through the tattered book for the parish priest, but what was his name? Paré? Picard? Poulin? Perhaps I should have shaken Maman awake. Perhaps I should have asked her right then for the names of all the priests in the city. Perhaps I should have cried out for Ste. Thérèse to guide me.

I decided I should simply pray. I would speak to God alone, without anyone to interpret for me. I lowered myself to my knees, and the black-and-white tiles seemed to tilt. I squeezed my eyes shut and tried to remember how to pray. It had been too long since I'd been to Mass, to confession.

In the dusk-lit hallway I opened my eyes to the surrounding dimness and relived the awe that had surrounded me just moments before, when Daphne had reached up and laughed. Ste. Brigid had been looking down on us. But now it seemed she had forgotten us, that we had much less, and the crush of this reality made me clasp my hands together more tightly and whisper uneven and erratic prayers. I knelt in the cold hallway and the chill of the tiles seeped straight through my legs and upwards, directly to my heart.

Above the phone table, a crucifix made of burnished gold, no bigger than a pencil, leaned out from the wall. I stood and took it down. Tracing the diminutive length of Jesus, I gazed at his beatific, pious face and his outstretched arms. Such a calm face. I held Him in my fingers and dialed the phone with his stiff pointed feet, each number circling back, then around again. Seven numbers for that local call. Seven sins, seven wonders of the world, seven sacraments peeling away at my soul. Jesus kicked his way around the circular dial. In one hand, I held the receiver to my ear, and in the other, the crucifix.

I imagined Mary's poor mother, trying to rest her worn-out back as the phone rang and rang, her daughter not home to answer. I rested the receiver back in its cradle and then held my ear to the wall, half expecting to hear divine murmurs of the saints from within the hollows between plaster and framework. What I heard was silence, so I pressed my cheek harder against the wallpaper. And there they were, my longing and my imagining. The novenas Mary offered up, the whispered words of the confessional, the lines of Latin that graced the priest's lips each Mass, rising and falling, traced with misfortune, mild and then tragic. And there, too, the sense of something further, just out of reach, scented with incense and dust and eventual, permanent quiet.

Jesus gazed up from my palm, much too serene to understand my suffering. I placed Him back at his station on the wall. Perhaps from the alcove He could watch for signs and saints, angels and first stars.

I recalled all the instances when friends and neighbors had uttered His name: "Jesus, Lord, bless us and preserve us." When Mary at age seven told her family about the blessing of our paper fleet, they didn't wave the story away. They believed in such things; they had the kind of faith that came wrapped for glory. Miracles draped themselves over our lives like fine, weighted fabric.

Things happened now and then at the Trinity Lanes: a pair of fisherman's boots had been left one night in lane number three, and our cat was found curled up and sleeping in a mound of odd-sized bowling shoes, surrounded by sand and shrimp heads; a week later a knotted-up blue crab net was found slung over a scoring table; and, on the ninth day after the ladies in the senior league started saying novenas, flotation cushions turned up under each and every bowling ball like babies' beds. Mary believed these were practical jokes, that is, until the ten pins in lane seven appeared each Thursday evening with the faces of the Apostles cast upon them. It looked as though they spoke amongst each other, and sometimes they watched as bowlers came forward to the lines of neighboring lanes. It was terrible for business and the leagues.

At first, no one wanted to bowl at all. But after a few weeks, Mary called in the bishops to sanctify the lane. She told me they entered the bowling alley in ivory robes with gold overlay, carrying incense and vessels of holy water. A velvet rope was placed at the end of the lane to cordon it off, and from then on, the place was packed. The regulars soon became accustomed to all the new visitors who wanted to check out the holy rollers. Someone noticed that Simon and Andrew were missing, there being only ten pins, and a bowler from the Lakeside League laughed and said, "Yeah, they must be out in the Gulf with the shrimping fleet." Ladies crossed themselves and even the men muttered a few prayers before sending balls down the open lanes.

Until then, Mary had watched for miracles. Now she lived smack in the middle of them. I needed her wide-open eyes. I needed the assistance of humanity more than that of the thin, unanswering Jesus before me. In the darkening hallway, He didn't call to me. There was a sad, meager air about Him. He seemed regretful. I switched on the light, and He remained inert and sorrowful in the astonishing brightness. Still, He had that look of serenity as well. Regret and sorrow? Peace and penitence? These were murky places where I had no business.

I imagined my parents standing there in the hallway, their clothes damp with brackish water, their gaze gray with wonder at the life I'd taken on. Motherhood, sacrilege, an unmarried state of affairs, their wide eyes and tight mouths seemed to say. But in truth, they were silent, unspeaking ghosts drowned long ago, the only sound that of their dripping scarves, the sharp metallic odor of seaweed rising from their pockets and from the pools around their shoes.

I shook them from my mind and went to wake Maman.

In her room, the curtains were drawn tight, the darkness dense and complete. I found the bedside lamp, and a triangle of yellow light fell over my sleeping grandmother. Her breath was still and even, and she looked more tranquil than the hallway Jesus. The satin edging of her wool blanket lay against her shoulder, and her cheek was pale in the lamplight. Years before, her hair had been dark and thick; now it fell across her face in thin, gray strands. I pushed it back, and her eyes fluttered but didn't open.

Eleven years before, her expression serene, her shoulder-length black hair twisted gently into a bun, Maman Yvette had sat in St. John's Cathedral beside my parents. I watched her as I came up the aisle behind Mary, walking the length of the church to receive our first Holy Communion, our white dresses whispering, our sashes tied into enormous bows. Maman's smile made her seem even younger; she was the youngest grandmother there. When I tripped on the last step before the altar, forgot most of my vows, swallowed too much of the offered wine and then coughed on the priest's vestments, Maman was not angry. She was happy for my soul. Once I'd received the wafer, round as a pastille and thin as a dime, insubstantial as a first ray of morning light, from then on I would go straight to heaven no matter what. Unconvinced that I would ever feel saved, I still felt a sense of contentment that Maman's mind was at ease.

The doorbell rang. A long, insistent ring. Maman sat up and blinked at me.

"Why, chère," she said. "You got your baby with you. She looks just like your mama did when she was a baby." Smiling, she reached out as if to hold Daphne.

Her words went through me, shining and cold, like silver chalices filled with lies. I held on to her words, afraid she would fall into the space that now held my child. It seemed there was another dimension, a place that swallowed us up, that took us away from one another. There was no way on earth I could bear to lose them both, my only family. I grasped Maman's hands, shaking them, trying to make her see what was happening.

"Maman," I said loudly, "I don't have Daphne." My tears came now, hot and torrential, like the meanest of summer rains. Had Maman gone around the bend to a place where she could see lost babies? I couldn't see her for all the fearsome weeping that had laid into me, but I felt her hands patting mine and I heard her voice.

"It's gonna be okay, chère," she said. "It's gonna be just fine. Don't you worry yourself like that. This baby here is a sure sign."

The bell chimed again. This time short and shrill. Loud knocking followed. Then a woman's voice called out. The knocking continued, and Maman nodded and motioned for me to go on and answer the door.

As I walked out into the hallway, I could see Mary through the front door's leaded glass. She stood next to an old man. Waving at me through the window, looking more desperate than excited, she cried, "Antoinette, open the door!"

"I'm coming," I said and pulled the door wide. The sudden scent of roses entered the hall, and the redolence called up cemetery vaults, garden walls, church altars, fractured sidewalks.

"Antoinette," Mary said, reaching for my shoulders, embracing me. "Look at you. After all these years, finally crying. But everything will be all right. I brought you a miracle."

"What?" I wiped my eyes with the heels of my palms and looked at the white-haired man. He seemed familiar.

We all stood in the doorway for a moment. Silent, staring. Nightfall around us.

"Bless my soul," called Maman from the hallway. She took one step at a time, holding Daphne with one arm and touching the wallpaper with the other. She followed the floral pattern and gently clutched my baby, my baby girl. And then I heard the old man speaking, and a puzzling reassurance settled over me.

"Yvette," he said, a slow, deep quality to his voice. Something about it reminded me of a voice heard over water.

"Cy Andrew," said Maman. "Why, I haven't seen you since you worked at the fish market. Some years gone by, nah? What reached out and brought you here?" She gazed at Mary, who was now looking hard at Daphne.

"Ha," said Daphne, her dimpled hands outstretched.

"Lord, child," said Maman. "Daphne, don't lean too far. I'll go and fall down in this here hallway." Grabbing onto the spindled back of a chair, she sat suddenly and settled Daphne in her lap, then kissed her small sweet fingers, one by one.

The foyer felt different, filled with our breathing. The hallway led not only to our home, but also toward Daphne's sudden wholeness. I moved toward Maman and my baby, who reached for me and then grabbed the collar of my blouse as I took her in my arms.

"Oh, it's my girl," I said. "That's right, Daph," I told her. "Hold on tight."

Daphne wriggled and then caught the side of my face with a tiny fingernail. I could feel the thin cut across my cheek. Propping her up onto my hip, I found myself praying silently to Ste. Brigid and Ste. Thérèse, even St. Valentine and the Blessed Virgin herself for my healthy baby, my absolute child.

As I stood next to Maman, my baby held close, I tried to imagine my life as any different. If Val had come home and married me, if my parents were still alive, if Daphne had never disappeared. But life didn't give those things; I had what I was meant to have. The church, the absence of men, a city below sea level but aboveboard when it came to what truly mattered. Babies, oyster loaves, grandmothers. Smiles, friends, beignets. A toss of beads at Carnival. Even the thinnest Communion wafer, there to remind of what was to come. My life couldn't be otherwise; it was what it was. Thank the hallway Jesus, thank the alcove that He filled, in the great wide scheme of things, it was what it was.

"Heaven on earth. Is that baby as fine as ever?" said Mary. She touched Daphne's tiny hands with the tips of her fingers, and Daphne began to wail.

I jostled her a little. "Hey, baby girl," I said, feeling her in my arms.

"I brought over Mr. Andrew," said Mary, her voice twisted with worry. "To help. I thought he could help." Her words became faint, almost a whisper.

Afraid to admit what I'd been through, afraid to confess that, yes, I'd been as lost as ever, I chose not to tell. There was just no way that I could explain Daphne's disappearance, as mysterious and sudden as her reappearance. If I gave in and admitted my fear, I'd give in to that other world. I'd somehow mar the perfection of the world as it now was, deflect the grace of God and send it reeling backward.

And so I said to Mary, "She's fine. Just like I told you. You see, it doesn't help to worry about things that will most likely right themselves in the end." Mary's shoulders shook; she was now the one crying. I pulled my friend close and hugged her, and Daphne squirmed between us. And then I did admit something. "This is truly a miracle," I said, my voice thin and wavering.

"That Daphne has always been your miracle, Antoinette," said Maman. "Since the very beginning. Ain't that so?"

"Oui, Maman," I answered and brushed my hand against hers.

Mr. Andrew smiled at us, and I noticed a brown paper sack in his hand. Our saintly fishmonger handed Maman the parcel.

"You brought me some catfish, Cy?" said Maman, looking up at him. "You want me to fix your supper, nah?"

She laughed like I hadn't heard her laugh in a long while.

Mary was busy counting Daphne's fingers and toes. "Lord, oh, Lord," she said. "I was so worried about this child."

She followed me as I walked through the open door out onto the porch and faced the January sky, a deep dark blue swept with thin gray clouds. Daphne nestled against me, and I drew my cardigan around her bare legs. In that glimpse of sky, the first star reached out, all alone.

"I know where I've seen Cy Andrew before," I said. "That day we were out here after the flood, sailing those paper boats. He was the man in the pirogue."

"That's right," said Mary.

"So he's not a saint?"

"Don't go fooling with me." Mary clasped her hands together, pleading.

"I'm sorry," I said. "I know you were scared."

"It's all right. Now let's go in so this baby doesn't get chilled. I don't know what I'd do if she got sick after all this."

But instead, I walked down the steps and waved to the neighbors who were coming home or sitting on their stoops watching the evening settle.

"Antoinette," Mary called behind me. "Why do you insist on getting on my last nerve? Come on back inside."

I glanced at her and smiled, then hitched Daphne higher on my hip and followed the sidewalk to the corner, to that cranny where the petite cluster of roses still grew, bright and unbothered. In the center a red one unfurled, its petals layered and complicated and yearning to be taken.

SOON THE FIRST STAR

What Celia would remember were the steps—on and on, upward, almost infinite. Kneeling, her chin atop the passenger seat, she gazed out the back window as the little car pulled away from the curb. The Capitol building— steps and more steps, columns, a glint of sunset in its gold dome—grew smaller and disappeared in the distance. The bright sky leaned into evening, and layers of darkness edged in, framed by the Karmann Ghia's windows like a picture, a tiny square of what it really was.

In the car a crumpled map lay on one side of the emergency brake, the thin black lever that Celia knew never to touch. Since she and her mother lived in a part of Florida where there weren't many hills and slopes, the brake was seldom an issue. It remained straight-on, another horizontal line in their flat little town. But now they were traveling, and in Tallahassee hills led to more hills, which gave a whole new meaning to views and looking up and emergency brakes.

Beside her, her mother pulled a slim cigarette out of its crinkly package. Celia loved the smell of cigarettes just before they were lit, the sound of the pack's crisp cellophane, and the image on the package: a triangle of white beside a triangle of light blue sky with clean white clouds. These were familiar things. Her mother flicked open the top of her silver lighter (one of the things Celia's father had left behind, one that was still useful) and leaned slightly forward into the flame.

"What you thinking, baby?" Her mother exhaled and glanced at Celia.

"Nothing, Mama," Celia said, lying because she was always thinking.

The December evening turned in on itself, black and starry. Celia was accustomed to wide-open beach skies, where at night ocean and sky became one. Here in northern Florida the stars were fringed and sometimes hidden by tall spiky pines and the earth's sudden curves. Celia wrapped her small hands inside the hem of her sweater.

"How come Daddy lives up here?"

"He lives in the house where his own mama and daddy once lived. Out in the country."

Celia leaned her head against the passenger window and felt the cold hard glass. Her mother tired easily of questions. She tried to smooth them over, the same way she smoothed the bed sheets each morning.

"But your daddy and I are going to fix some things, okay?" Her mother held a hand out to Celia, and the small gold chain of her wristwatch caught for a second in a loose stitch of Celia's sweater.

"What things?"

"Oh, just things," her mother said. "Some mistakes."

Celia thought of the beach where they lived and all the mistakes she'd ever made. Going to the water's edge without a grown-up, leaving her sandy shoes on inside the house, crying about the sand spurs that pricked her bare feet when she walked through the yard. She imagined her mother's mistakes as seagulls with broken wings, unable to fly, falling sideways into the sea.

"There are some things I did when your daddy left. He left in such a hurry, and you were so little." Her mother sighed. "You're still too little for me to be telling you this."

Celia recalled how her father had read poetry aloud to her mother. How her mother would lie back on the couch and listen, and Celia, still awake in her room, would listen too. Words like *chicory, daisies, restlessness*—words so pretty, so odd and ordered, still echoed inside her.

Through the car window, Celia looked up at the stars and the whir of black outside. She wanted to lie on the side of the road, on the shoulder where the grass grew high, and find Cassiopeia, the wide bright "W" in the night sky. She imagined asking her mother to stop. But she didn't ask, and they continued on along Interstate 90, through the outskirts of Tallahassee, past the exits for Sneads and Altha, and on toward a place called Marianna.

At this time of year, Celia should have been in her first-grade class in school with the other six-year-olds, spelling and adding and planting fat white beans in little milk cartons full of black dirt. But her mother hadn't driven her to school that morning. They'd headed in the opposite direction, stopping for breakfast and lunch, once at a filling station, and a few times at places her mother said looked pretty but then didn't bother getting out of the car to see.

On the backseat a small suitcase bounced around when the Karmann

Ghia hit occasional ruts in the road. The suitcase was two-tone, light and dark brown, with gold clasps that snapped shut. When she was younger, Celia had loved to open and close this suitcase, just to hear the neat clicks and pops of the shiny clasps, so definite and precise. The time she'd pinched a finger in the space between the clasps, her father quickly opened the case and held her finger to his lips. "It was the baby finger," he said softly, kissing away the hurt.

Her mother reached over and brushed Celia's cheek with the tips of her fingers. Celia smelled smoke and perfume.

"You're so quiet sometimes that I just have to make sure you're still there."

She turned to her mother and thought to herself, "Why?"

Her mother turned on the heater. Warm air blew around inside the car, and Celia's fine hair fluttered away from her face. The car hummed along, its edgy little motor a background to the song her mother sang under her breath. The song sounded familiar. Something about land and skies and never any fences. The tune was sure, but the words floated out of reach.

"When are we going to get there?" Celia asked.

"Too soon," her mother said. She gave Celia a quick look. "I mean, in a little while, baby. Do you want to lie down in back?"

Celia glanced behind at the suitcase. "No, that's okay. I'll just stay up here." She leaned against her seat and tried to find another constellation. The sky zoomed by, an inky blur. Her eyes closed, and she gave in to sleep.

When her father said good-bye, Celia was days away from her fifth birthday. She'd thought he was coming back. Her mother's friend, Nicky, arrived that afternoon, just like she did every time he left. Time after time, whether her father was gone for days or weeks, Nicky would be there in the doorway, a grocery sack clutched in one hand and a look on her face that fell somewhere between dismay and duty. She strode into the kitchen and started cooking and, when there were several meals stacked up on the shelves of the Frigidaire, she would clean the house. She called Celia's father "the man," and if he hadn't returned, she'd either stay a while longer or pull Celia's mother out of bed and sit her down and make her get a handle back on life.

"You got a child now, Blythe, honey," she'd say. "You can't just spend your days bemoaning the fact the man is gone. Besides, you know he'll be home soon."

Back then, he had always returned. Not this time, though. This time he'd packed a big suitcase full of clothes and books. But he'd left some things behind: his sterling lighter, his collection of diner mugs, a book of poetry by William Carlos Williams, and his name—Lane Daniels—inscribed on the lighter and in the book.

This time he hadn't left in the middle of the night. After breakfast, he washed the cups and plates, put away the butter and the syrup, and kissed Mama on the top of her head. She didn't look up when he said good-bye. Celia followed him through the house, and at the front entrance he leaned down and cupped her chin in one hand. "I'll be seeing you in my dreams, little C." The screen door slammed, and the bright morning sun fell over the hallway in broad, dusty sweeps. The day became dull and warm, and Celia remembered her mother lying in a bed of rumpled sheets for hours at a time, broken dishes scattered throughout the house, the radio turned up loud.

That same afternoon Celia had called Nicky, dialing the numbers on the yellow telephone in the living room. She knew the numbers by heart now. Nicky drove over and left her old car idling in the driveway. She looked down at the floors covered in ivory shards, some of the bases and handles of the mugs still intact, leaned her head into Celia's parents' bedroom, and then pulled the door shut. Celia stood there in the hallway. In one tightly closed hand, she held the corner of a feather pillow, and an overnight bag spilled its contents around her sneakered feet.

Nicky led Celia outside, lifted her into the white Pontiac, and fastened a thread-worn lap belt around her. As Nicky backed her car slowly toward the street, Celia searched the deep interior for the parking brake and felt relieved not to find one. The only things she could reach were the radio dials, which only spun in place. They drove past Ponce Inlet and then down to Nicky's cottage at the other end of New Smyrna Beach, stopping just once at a filling station for soft drinks.

When they arrived at Nicky's house, Celia felt the day stand still. She stood in the kitchen next to Nicky, holding onto her flowered dress and an empty 7-Up bottle. The windows were open, and a breeze pushed the curtains into the room. Celia could hear the waves outside.

"Let loose of my clothes now," Nicky said. She pulled at the clutch of material that Celia held onto. "It's gonna be fine, Celia. You hear?"

Celia dropped the glass bottle, and it rolled across the linoleum. She looked up into Nicky's brown eyes and tried her best to believe her, but still she clung to the dress.

A few days later Nicky made a chocolate cake. On the kitchen table were raspberry ice cream and gifts too. It was Celia's birthday. A few of Nicky's neighbors came with gumdrops and pink balloons that floated from strings, but there were no children at her party, and neither of her parents arrived to help her blow out the candles.

Days and then weeks went by and still Celia stayed with Nicky, who wore tortoiseshell combs in her hair and rarely rested herself when she made Celia lie down in the afternoons. Nicky spent most days whipping up desserts and washing clothes. And three days each week, in the evenings, they'd drive up South Atlantic Avenue past all the number streets to North Atlantic, delivering baskets of clean laundry and fresh-baked pies and cakes. They never stopped to check in on Celia's mother, and Celia didn't ask to see her. The people they met never questioned why Celia now rode with Nicky. They simply thanked Nicky and sometimes offered Celia twists of licorice.

Celia preferred the roads closer to Nicky's house, where the neighbors sat on their porches and called out, "Good evening, Miss Nicky!" and "Hey there, Celi!" There, the land narrowed with ocean on one side and bay on the other, and the roads were named for different kinds of fish—Mullet, Sheepshead, Catfish, Snook, Starfish. Even the narrowest streets were named. Even the dead-end street, dotted with little houses—pink, coral, and orange cottages where fishermen and their families lived and where the beach leveled out into the thick scrub of the national seashore. Nicky's house was flamingo pink and raised up on stilts for the times when the high tides reached past the dunes, edging all the backyards. Nicky's yard was surrounded by tall, knotted saw grass and crossed by lines of linens waving in the constant wind.

The summer before, Celia's father and mother had brought her here—to visit Nicky and to spend the days fishing. They'd caught pompano, and Nicky had baked the fish whole inside a paper bag. Celia had gotten sunburned, and her mother had covered her in Noxzema cold cream, which cooled her skin and made her feel loved. She remembered, too, how her father had held her up high on his shoulders so that she could be nearer to the sky. She'd stretched small fingers toward the clouds, a line of pelicans, and the red kite that was a dot against the clear blue.

Celia noticed that no one flew kites now. Too cold, too windy these late autumn days. Nicky's swept-up hair fell from its combs and billowed out in wisps, like the dark fishing nets Celia had seen the neighboring fishermen cast into the surf.

Once, out on the tideline they found a scallop shell, perfect, still attached at the wings. Celia held it out for Nicky to see, its round rosy form echoing the shape and color of her small palm. Nicky reached down in the wet sand and brought up a moon snail, its exterior whorled with brown and cream colors and its door shut tight.

"Your mama loved collecting moon snails when we were growing up together," Nicky said. "She would keep them overnight in a pail filled with sand and seawater and the next morning she'd lay them out on the porch."

Celia touched the snail's shell with one finger and traced its fat curves. She stared up at Nicky, at the soft lines around her eyes, and frowned. She didn't like to think of her mother these days. Just beyond them, a sanderling fished in the shallows.

"What?" Nicky said. "You haven't ever done that? To see if they still crawl?"

Celia dug her feet along the wet sand, narrow trails appearing and disappearing as the tide continued to roll in. "No," she said, looking down as saltwater lapped around her ankles.

In the evenings after supper, Nicky and Celia played the brand-new Scrabble game that Celia had unwrapped on her birthday. No one was there to ask, "Isn't she a bit young?" Celia loved the wooden squares, each with its own neat black letter and tiny scoring number. The possibilities for finding words, all jumbled up in a box. Words like *sun*, *moon*, and *cream* crossed paths with *socks*, *cat*, and *kiss*. Celia won three games in a row and Nicky said, "Well, I give up. You're way too smart for me, Celia Daniels." She patted her lap, and Celia found a place to sit and be held. Celia laid her head back against Nicky's shoulder and listened to the ocean rush in and rush out beyond the wide porch windows.

At the end of a rainy day, as the clouds eased off to the south, Nicky set the kitchen table with baskets of fried chicken and cream biscuits, smothered greens, and a fancy sweet potato pie. Celia ran into the kitchen and grabbed Nicky around the waist. Nicky hugged back, saying, "Whoa now, Celi. Slow right on down."

"But Nicky," Celia said, in a tone just shy of whining.

"You know better than that. 'But Nicky,' my soul. Hand me that pie now."

"Is it shoofly pie?"

"You are something. No such thing as shoofly pie in this house. We gonna have a good supper, though. Your mama's coming too."

"What for?" Celia knotted her brow, feeling mean. She didn't want to see her mother or share Nicky.

"Miss Celia Daniels," Nicky said in a hushed voice. "Your mama is coming here tonight, and you will be a good girl."

"Yes, ma'am." Celia held one hand behind her back and crossed her fingers. Nicky reached around and gently pulled the fingers apart.

"I told you, you know better than to fool, young miss."

Celia held out her empty hands, and Nicky gently clasped them between her own.

"You know, I once had a little girl." Nicky sat down and pulled Celia to her side. "So I know all about things little girls do."

"Where is she now?" Celia asked.

"She went off with her daddy one day. Out in the fishing boat. Storm came up and took them." She placed her hands over Celia's shoulders. "I don't fret though. I don't have time to fret in this world. I'll just wait until I get to the next one."

Wet, heavy air pushed into the room. Celia felt the weight of Nicky's hands and imagined them holding her down, keeping her from drifting away. "What was her name?"

Nicky looked past Celia, and Celia turned to see what she was looking at. The window screens were streaked from the day's rains. Beyond, the sky was spun with gray light.

"Her name was Dinah. I always loved that song about sitting in the kitchen with Dinah—you know that song? She was always in the kitchen with me."

"Oh," Celia said.

"Now go wash your hands for supper."

In the bathroom Celia turned the silver faucet handle and felt the cold water splash onto her hands, smelled the sweet white soap, and eased the lather up to her wrists. She wondered how old Dinah had been when she went out in the boat. A frayed towel hung beside the sink, and Celia dried her hands.

In the next room the phone was ringing.

"I'm coming, I'm coming," Nicky said, as she hurried to answer it, nearly running into Celia as she came out of the bathroom. And then, "Hey, Blythe. Where you at? Food's on the table." A long pause made Nicky bend over the phone, and then she said, "Mm-hmm. Well, all right, we'll look for you tomorrow then."

Celia wasn't surprised. She already knew that her mother wouldn't come. She and Nicky ate together, just as they had in the past weeks. The chicken was seasoned with salt and pepper, and the biscuits doused with butter, and the pie served with extra whipped cream. They didn't talk about Celia's mother; instead, they sang a little and waved their drumsticks in the air to keep time.

Before bedtime they walked out onto the damp beach and looked at the stars. Celia craned her neck and whirled around, looking for a single star. Always alone, bright but tangled in the breadth of surrounding constellations, the blur of cloud trails, Andromeda shone, light years away, secure in the enormous sky.

"Why are there so many, Nicky?" asked Celia, leaning back against Nicky's skirts. "I get dizzy trying to see them all."

"Listen, doll, the stars are soul-dust. Someday you'll get to be a star, too, looking down instead of up."

Nicky squeezed Celia's small hand, and they walked back to the house. Celia thought about how her mother would come the next day in their sky-blue car, how she'd wear a bright kerchief and sunglasses, and how she'd lean down for a kiss. Celia slid her sandy feet between the sheets and fell asleep.

* * *

More than a year had passed since those days with Nicky in south New Smyrna. Celia awoke now to murmurs and dim shadows in a room she didn't know. Even the covers around her felt strange. As her eyes adjusted, she saw patterns sewn into the quilt—spirals and circles. Then she recognized the voice. It was deep and soft, like the brown wool vest he used to wear. She sat up and heard her mother's voice too. The voices blended as if they belonged together, two tones of the same song.

"She's much taller now. She is six, after all." Her mother's voice, a nervous laugh surrounding her words. "And she still asks questions. I know I disappoint her. Sometimes I don't even try to find answers."

After a moment, her father's voice, hesitant. "Is she six already?"

Celia pushed the covers away. She swung her feet out of the bed and then stopped. They stood together in the doorway, looking in, just like they used to every night at bedtime.

"Celia?" It was her mother who whispered her name. "You awake, baby?"

Celia looked up, and her father responded with a gentle step forward.

"Hey, Celia." Her father softly spoke her name. The moment stumbled forward. Later, Celia would remember it as fleeting, a lissome second, like a flower blown away, buried by sand.

Her mother remained in the doorway, the hall light illuminating her hair, the outline of her black sweater. Celia kneaded the sleep from her eyes and looked over at her father's face. He seemed tired and distracted. He made a motion that she was used to, running his hand through his hair, which was still blond and wavy. Celia remembered how he swept it back as the wind on the beach tried to blow it forward. It never stayed though; the wind always won, leaving it standing stiff, in all directions. "A perfect mess," her mother would say.

As he came closer, Celia tilted her head and pulled on a section of her hair, twisting it hard. Her father sat on the edge of the bed, a little away from her, and held out a hand. There was uncertainty in the gesture. Celia twisted the lock of hair even tighter. Eyes wide, mouth set, she had to protect herself from fathers who left, from mothers who stayed but weren't really there. Her father's hand still reaching for hers, Celia held out her own. Past them, the doorway threw a triangle of light into the room, her mother no longer there.

Friday, the night Celia and her mother had arrived, lapsed into Saturday, and Saturday fell into Sunday. A weekend moving slowly, its edges indistinct, undefined. Sunday morning seemed an entire day, its seconds creeping forward. Celia looked out the open window that faced the side yard and a bend of road just past the tree line. A slender anole sunned itself on the ledge, its curved green body breathing, eyes closed. An inside door slammed. Celia started, and the lizard slipped over the ledge, a glimpse of tail and gone.

"Celia, I've been looking for you, baby." Her mother stood next to her. The moment became unquiet. "Remember on the way here, how I explained some things?"

Celia remembered what her mother had said in the car, about fixing things. She pulled at the loose thread on her sweater and said nothing. She watched her mother's mouth, the words hard and brittle, like little sticks.

"We'll go to the courthouse in Tallahassee tomorrow, okay?"

Celia traced the windowsill with her fingers and nodded.

"After your daddy left, I was so angry I made sure he couldn't come back. But now I know I was wrong." Her mother pushed Celia's bangs away from her brow. "You need to see your daddy sometimes."

The morning drifted in between her mother's words. Celia pushed away from the window and walked barefoot into the hallway. Her mother followed her, still talking all too quietly, explaining that something called a protective order would have to be lifted, that a judge could do that for them.

"Do you understand, Celia?"

Celia leaned against a set of grooves in the wood paneling. The wall gave a bit. "I'm hungry," she said.

In the kitchen Celia sat down at the small dinette table and examined the pattern in the tabletop. She wondered if the judge would wear black robes, if he would lift the order above their heads, if the order would be much too heavy to lift.

"Hey there, C," her father said. He placed a bright yellow plate on the table in front of her. Three pancakes, not too big, not too small, sat on the plate, syrup trickling down and around.

"Pecan?" Celia asked, her nose crinkling.

"Thought you might still like them."

"Here, baby," her mother said, as she set a glass of milk on the table. "Eat up now."

"Aren't you eating, Mama?"

"Oh, I had something already." She pulled her pack of cigarettes from the pocket of her slacks. Tucked into the cellophane sleeve was the silver lighter. Her mother glanced up at her father, who was flipping another pancake, his back to her. Celia watched her mother stuff the cigarettes back into her pocket and leave the room. She knew her mother hadn't eaten anything. She seemed to live on air, or smoke.

Her father turned from the stove and set down a large orange platter. It was stacked with more griddlecakes, speckled with chopped pecans and steaming, the scent of cinnamon wafting through the room. He hummed as he poured coffee into one of the diner mugs he collected, this one ivory with yellow stars splashed around the rim. Celia stared at the stars as he put the mug to his lips and swallowed.

"You forgot your mugs, the ones on the kitchen shelf. At home," Celia said, blinking at her father. "There's the green one, and the blue one with white mice running all around its sides, and some plain white ones too."

"Yeah, I did. I guess I thought—" He clasped the mug before him—a new one. "Well, it doesn't matter. Don't you use them?"

"No," Celia answered. "We don't." Her mouth was full, her words heavy and dull. "Mama broke some." She gazed up at her father and waited. "And I can't reach them."

That evening they sat in lawn chairs outside in the yard. It was clear, a crisp star-filled night, almost Christmas. Bordered by sycamore, elm, and pecan trees, the land was unclouded by the taller, scruffier pines so usual up this way. Trumpet creepers wound their way around the largest trees' trunks. Celia's mother sang to herself, that same song. Never any fences. Her father leaned forward in his chair, watching her mother, and sang over her words.

"Give me land, lots of land under starry skies above."

Celia's mother gave her father a look, and her father returned the look, but smiled and continued singing.

Celia sat against the laced back of her chair, kicking at the air under her feet. Her mother smoked, and her father looked out at the sky. A breeze sounded in the trees; it felt too quiet now that her father had stopped singing. The words were his, too, thought Celia, not just her mother's. He was the one with the big backyard full of stars and pecan trees. Her mother had only leftover cups on her shelf. And the lighter.

"It's Cassiopeia, C." Her father pointed north, a shining "W" at his fingertips. "It's good she has a chair too."

"A throne," Celia's mother said, her voice clouded by cigarette smoke.

"Nicky calls her Queen Cassie, sitting way up there on her rocking chair," Celia said, trying to imitate Nicky's drawl.

"How is Nicky?" Celia's father asked.

"Why don't you come down sometime and ask her yourself?" Celia's mother said. "I'm sure she'll tell you."

Her father looked across her, as if she wasn't there, directly at Celia. "Does Nicky still tell you stories?"

Celia hesitated. Her mother's remark tumbled through the air, unforgotten and bitter. "She always tells the one about Little Andy," Celia said. "About how her mama and daddy chain her to that big rock, and how the horrible sea-monster wants to eat her up."

"But he doesn't, does he?" her father said.

Celia tucked up her feet, knees under her chin. "Nicky never tells the end 'cause she says it hasn't happened yet. She says you can't know the end if it hasn't happened."

"Right," her father said. "You can't."

Celia glanced at her mother, who threw up her hands as if to say, "You're asking me?" Her truer response was the trail of smoke from the end of her cigarette.

When Celia looked back to her father's chair, he wasn't there, and the back door bumped shut.

It was Monday morning, so early that Celia could see the sun lift itself over the treetops, as round and bright as her father's big yellow plates. The sunlight fell through the kitchen windows and shimmered over the fine blond hairs of Celia's arms. She reached across the table for her breakfast. There were scrambled eggs, sunny and feather-light, with bacon and toast. A small, thick-bottomed blue cup filled with orange juice for Celia, two large white mugs of coffee for her parents. Her father's mug read "Sal's Diner" in wavy green writing. Her mother's was circled around the rim with a thin red line, no words. Her mother nibbled at the corners of her toast, then excused herself.

"She never eats," Celia said loudly, hoping her mother would hear. If she heard, she might come back and sit down and finish her eggs.

Celia's father put down his fork. His arms rested on the tabletop, and his gaze followed the sounds of Celia's mother in the next room. "No, she doesn't, does she?" he said.

"Oh, where are they?" Celia's mother asked.

From the kitchen, they heard exasperated tones, things falling. Celia's mother searching for cigarettes. Then the front door slammed, and the Karmann Ghia backed down the dirt driveway, the reverse gear whining in an insistent, determined way. Celia's father stood up and walked quickly to the door.

"It's okay, Daddy," Celia said, following her father into the living room.

He opened the door, its dark pine giving way to the morning outside. Celia stood beside him and looped her arm into the crook of his elbow. The sun was brighter now. Celia had to squint to see the little car, a blue dot speeding along the road.

Celia's mother didn't come back. At noon her father called Nicky, explaining things, leaning into the telephone and trying to cover his words with his hand. From her place at the kitchen table, Celia stared up at him, absently clinking her empty cup against her mother's plate.

"Why does she do these things, Nicky?" he said. "No, she left a few hours ago." He held the phone in one hand, his brow hidden by tousled hair, the other hand twisting the cord. "Right." He took a long breath. "I know all about the court orders. I've been living up here because of them, haven't I? Look, I'd appreciate it if you'd try to see things from— What? I don't know. Well, by now we've missed our meeting. Dammit, Nick, I know that!"

Celia slammed her cup into the plate. A long crack slid under her mother's uneaten toast. Startled, her father looked over at her, at the cup in her hand.

"I'll bring Celia to you then," her father said and laid the receiver back in its cradle.

They waited until late afternoon before leaving, just in case Celia's mother returned.

"I guess Mama got scared," Celia said, as she followed her father out to his red truck. White letters, spelling out F-O-R-D, had been painted on its tailgate years ago. Now they looked faded and worn, and a small dent accented the O.

Her father dropped the suitcase on the cab's bench seat. It bounced slightly, and Celia thought of her flannel pajamas all mixed up with her mother's striped slacks, the black sweater she'd left behind. She wondered if her mother was cold, wherever she was.

"Don't worry, Celia," her father said, as he lifted her up into the truck. "We'll see your mama soon."

Celia scooted across the seat's slippery vinyl upholstery, her feet barely grazing the floor. "And Nicky too," she said in one breath. "Right?" Nothing seemed sure now. Nothing except each moment clicking past, her father taking everything slowly, carefully. He looked at Celia, his gaze hopeful, almost promising.

"Right," he answered. He climbed into his side of the cab, pulled the heavy door closed, and positioned the shifter down towards himself. The truck headed out slowly. Behind them, pecan shells slid backwards in the rusted-out bed, while dried oak leaves blew about in shushed whispers under the wheels.

Celia sat up straight to see out of the large windshield and watched the winding road grow larger as they approached it from the driveway. She imagined her mother seeing the same world hours before, and she winced as the car accident happened inside her mind. The Karmann Ghia a scrap of blue at the side of the road, her mother crushed between the metal roof and the steering wheel. The parking brake still a flat line against the mangled car's curves.

When she'd stayed with Nicky, she told her about the bad scared thoughts she had, the ones she was afraid would come true. "We all have those crazy thoughts, baby doll. But you don't need to worry 'cause they stay right inside your head," Nicky had said, the palm of her hand resting on Celia's head.

The radio dial switched on under her father's fingers. A song about leaving by the Louvin Brothers. Her father pulled the tuner quickly to the left and there was the Twist. Celia reached for the supper her father had packed: cheese and lettuce sandwiches wrapped in waxed paper, bottles of Coca-Cola balanced between tart red apples and a bag of candied pecans that slid around on the seat. She held her sandwich and looked at the bend in the road up ahead. She wondered how her father could take such good care of her and then leave, driving away from her and reaching this very same road. And how her mother had such a hard time with taking care, and it was Nicky who cooked and cleaned and told stories. Now it was her mother who had left. It was new and she didn't like it. She felt cold and lonely even though she wore her button-down sweater, even though her father was sitting right next to her.

Soon the first star appeared. Her father pointed it out as they turned and swooped north for a second, stopping at an intersection, watching it blink back at them. Around the next corner, beyond its tiered and towering steps, the Capitol building rose up, just as it had a few days before. The sky was awash with color, dark indigo and sweeps of rose, the moon already high. Through the large truck window, the Capitol looked smaller than it had in her mother's car, the gold crown less prominent. Celia realized the judges had gone home to their own suppers, not the kind that was shared on a truck's bench. They had pulled their long night-black robes over their heads and hung them up on great brass hooks. They'd unlocked wooden cabinets with deep drawers and tucked all the orders away. For another time.

IF YOU ASK THEM NICELY

Minnows. **Fat, green minnows.** Lizzy tries to grab a smaller one and misses. The lake water is clear in the shallows. She stretches too far past the minnows and sand swirls up, a milk-white cloud. The fish disappear for a few seconds and then reveal themselves below cypress roots, out of reach.

Lizzy squats by the roots, and water inches up her bathing suit. The roots are like smooth, brown, tangled fingers. Reaching between, she doesn't think of the water moccasins that might be hiding, the ones that her cousin May says are there, waiting to bite with a fierceness beyond any ever known. Lizzy just wants a minnow.

"What are you doing?" asks May. She stands on the shore, hands on her hips, her smocked dress and bare feet dirty.

"You know what I'm doing," says Lizzy, frowning. "Looking for minnows. I almost had a baby one a minute ago. "

"I know how to catch the babies," says May. She leans forward and shades her eyes from the bright sun. "You want me to tell you how?"

Strips of birch bark litter the sand. One rests against May's ankle like a sandal strap. Beyond, the stand of trees reveals bald patches, a seven-year-old's small afternoon of work.

"No," Lizzy answers. "You shouldn't bother me. Nana said so."

"Well, I'm going tell you anyway. I'll tell you and then you can try it, okay?"

Tired of squatting, Lizzy stands. The minnows are too hard to reach with her hands, and she looks for a stick. Her swimsuit sags, and lake water drips from it. She glares at May. "You can do whatever you like, but you can't make me listen."

May strides into the shallows, her long, skinny legs sending the water in all directions. And then she stops and lingers. The water pools around her ankles as she observes her reflection, a wavering, white-blond child. Sunlight bleaches the lake, and May squints. Suddenly, she drops down and lies flat. Like sea grass, her dress floats and then slowly falls around her body. Lizzy stands over her, stifling an urge to kick. The air is still and hot.

"It's like a bathtub that Nana ran the tap for, see?" explains May. "You know how she barely fills it?"

May lies farther back, the lake level with her ears, and Lizzy steps over her, still looking for that stick.

"You just lay here real quiet-like," says May, "and the babies come to you. They come and start to nibble at your toes and fingers, like they're looking for meat. And then, just then, if you ask them nicely, they might even let you hold them in your palm."

After days of lazing on their grandmother's backyard beach, Lizzy knows exactly what May means. More than once, chin down in the sand, Lizzy has held her hands in the water and watched the little fish, their glassy eyes staring at nothing, their blue-green bodies wriggling around, tickling. She's seen their backbones right through them, gray-yellow with tiny notches.

"I call 'em miracle babies," says May.

Lizzy glances back at May. The afternoon sun shines through her cousin's knotted hair. Drifting on the water's surface next to May is the perfect stick. Lizzy crouches down and picks it up. She balances the slim wand of cypress between her fingers. Several drops of water fall onto the lake surface just above May and her smocked dress, the same dress she wore to the fair a few days earlier.

Multi-colored confetti lay scattered in the midway, imitating the raised polka dots of May's dress. When Nana gave each of the girls a quarter for treats, they decided on the bright sugar-spun candy that wound around a white paper cone. 50 cents, read the sign. A giant Ferris wheel revolved behind them, the sunset sky cherry-pink between the spokes and tilting seats, while the fat lady at the concessions stand twirled a gauzy web of burnt, flying sugar onto their cone. May held her hand out, her head angled in expectation, while Lizzy turned to watch the lights, the evening edging in.

A small child on the Ferris wheel screamed for the ride to stop. Farther out, clouds traced lines of violet across the fading daylight. The unmistakable smell of burning sugar swept around her, and for a single moment Lizzy felt lost, as though the twilight expanse would swallow her. Thoughts she usually pushed aside surfaced, spinning amidst the carnival lights and laughter. Missing fathers, desperate mothers, and the war that separated them. The blur of the wheel slowed to a sharp, distinct stop, and May nudged Lizzy, offering her the cotton candy. All that was left was a small, wadded stump of crushed pink at one side.

Lizzy's fingers tighten around the algae-covered stick. May rests in the lukewarm shallows, her eyes closed. Around her, minnows gather, slowly swimming into the spaces at the crooks of her elbows, the curve of her neck. Bright little fish, they surround May's body, encircling her shape, until there are so many minnows that they become May's shape, another May entirely. A cerulean, flitting, opaquely fishlike May.

Wisps of hair fall against Lizzy's brow as she tilts her head, considering her cousin, this day, so many days. The shoreline slants down past May into darker depths, where lily pads and weeds grow thick. May stole pennies; May lied that their fathers would return and their mothers would stop crying; May lingered over mean stories in the middle of the night. But she was always there.

Standing over her cousin, Lizzy feels certain and calm. May is as silent as the silver fish flickering around her. Mesmerized, Lizzy holds the stick away from her body, even with the horizon, and drops it into the water. A small, plunking splash, and the minnows explode from May. Like a star departing itself, luminous and bursting, they dart and flee, little particles, little miracles of another afternoon.

BOBWHITE

She'd turned nine in October of 1955, that year when presidents and mothers were sent to the hospital. Carly's father called the president Dwight instead of President Eisenhower, and he called his wife Vivienne instead of Mrs. Robicheaux. Carly paid attention to what her father said, especially when he called her by her given name: Caroline. Especially when her mother was driven to the Touro Infirmary and her father became a man of few words. He still began their bedtime ritual of reading from the worn volume of *Just-So Stories*, but after the first "O Best Beloved," a long pause came, and her father kissed her goodnight. She lay awake and imagined her mother swathed in white sheets and cotton blankets in a bed much narrower than the one she slept in at home; she did not imagine anything about the president. She did note, however, that both the president and her mother had to rest away from home, with doctors and nurses all around, because of similar ailments—ailments of the heart.

Carly also understood that little girls without mothers at home to care for them were sent away to relatives. That was the way things were done. Quietly, without exception. Swiftly, in the first light of morning, waking to the call of doves outside her bedroom window, then the click of latches—a worn leather suitcase filled with neatly folded dresses and dungarees, the tattered Kipling book, a handful of toys including a favorite nameless doll, a brush and comb set, all readied by her father. And since she couldn't take him with her, her father promised to take good care of Cushion, their teacup yorkie—even if it meant walking him every day to the small law firm where he worked—until Carly returned. There was no mention of her mother's return, only sighs and large hands pressed against her shoulders and strict hospital rules of "no children allowed" and unconvincing apologies of "when you're older, you'll understand."

Since her mother's illness had progressed and she'd arrived at Aunt Belle and Uncle Theo's, Carly didn't know what to make of things. Her aunt and uncle were kind, and their sixteen-year-old son, Robbie, though he kept to himself at first, made her feel welcome. Her aunt showed her the upstairs bedroom that would be all hers, tucked into a corner with windows all around and a thick yellow quilt on the bed. The big country house; the empty rooms; the time now spent alone rather than playing with friends or reading with her mother, Cushion nestled between them; the family, once distant, who gathered her into familiar arms—these things, these changes moved across the longwinded days like great, sweeping hands. Across the porch floor Carly scattered shiny jacks—two-sies and three-sies—and, like their little metal spines, her thoughts seemed to make the same repeated, rolling click.

The sky was wider there than in the city, where courtyards and heavy drapes and tree-lined streets kept the heavens from peering too closely. Days at home were spent indoors, out of the hot sun, or if outdoors at all, then in the stippled shade of banana leaves or in the swing under the large side-yard oak.

But in Picayune, Mississippi, life happened outdoors. The autumn afternoons had grown cooler, and a weary sort of color washed up against the sky as the evenings settled in. Uncle Theo and Robbie went off hunting, eventually returning around dusk with the deep pockets of their hunting vests filled with bobwhite quail, limp, but sometimes still warm. Mesmerized, Carly watched as the men moved through the ritual of covering the ground with soft brown feathers, filling a tin bowl with innards for the tired setters, and arranging the bodies on the woodpile stump. In the dim evening light, the mound of bird carcasses seemed like a sweet, sad predicament.

At times like this, Carly felt her brow tighten and her mouth pull into a thin line. This wasn't a feeling she could explain, but she knew by the expressions of those around her that her own expression had changed. When she looked in the mirror each morning to brush her chin-length hair, she'd practice a series of looks—eyes crossed, wise, stern, utterly unhappy—all the while considering her freckles and her small mouth and her unlovely tangles, the color of twigs. She frowned at her reflection and remembered how her mother would kiss away the creases that lined her forehead when she fell into deep thought. She wished she could do something in return, but her mother was back home under gauzy white hospital sheets in New Orleans, while Carly was far away, up in the woodlands of Mississippi.

* * *

There, in the country outside the quiet town of Picayune, Carly had begun to follow the rhythms of each day and slowly they became her rhythms. The city life that she had been accustomed to lingered in her limbs as she hurried herself to dress for school in the mornings. But gradually she eased into the days and each afternoon, once the school bus deposited her at the familiar dirt driveway, she looked forward to seeing her aunt gathering tomatoes, mirlitons, and handfuls of tarragon from the garden, and then watching for her cousin and uncle who usually arrived later. Right along where the large mound of azaleas grew, the three Irish Setters—Thelma, France, and Idle—came running and barking. They bounded through the yard together, a blur of large paws and brown eyes and burr-studded bodies, Carly laughing at the tangle of legs as the dogs beat her to the back door.

One late November afternoon, pushing through the screen door into the kitchen, Carly found Robbie home. He looked up at the swish of dogs' tails, then at Carly.

"Hey, Carly," he said. "You sure take your time, don't you?"

Breathless from running, she answered, "It's not me. It's that old bus driver. He slows down for just about everything."

She set her satchel of books down and walked over to the counter where her cousin arranged quail onto a metal tray. How small and naked they seemed. Glossy little things. Smooth, the color of pink pearls. So different from their feathered selves, or the roasted version served on a platter with sweet onions and carrots and sage. Carly knew their taste as rich and wild, the scent and flavor of the woodlands in them. And yet she questioned their transformation from living creatures with calls and warbles to still, silent weights inside the leather game bags. Considering the idea of hunting, of the birds as a kind of sport, rather than creatures meant simply to sing and roost and fly, she came to the conclusion that the whole thing was unfair and sad. She preferred to think of them as alive.

Trying to imitate the birds' sounds, she pursed her lips and tried to whistle. A low, hollow note sounded, and Robbie almost smiled. His expression resembled one that belonged to his father, who smiled to himself at times, but never seemed more than slightly amused at things that were, in Carly's mind, truly funny.

She remembered how, one evening, as she had watched the men sort and clean the game birds, Uncle Theo glanced over in her direction, perhaps concerned—at her somber expression or at the brittle situation of a girl so far from her mother—but then looked back to his work. The sun had begun to fall backwards over the treetops. Her uncle moved in an unhurried, measured way, unlike his younger brother, Carly's father, who'd lived in the city far too long to be leisurely. Tall and stooped, Uncle Theo managed his height with a manner of elegance known to country gentlemen. His hair had begun to gray, and the light blue of his eyes had a rare quality, like the sky on a cloudless day. Carly pictured her uncle's thoughts threading along cautiously by the way he spoke to her and Robbie, as if considering every utterance and every pause would do less harm to the world.

Robbie was quiet, too, but his unspoken thoughts seemed to burden the air around him. Still, he was not unkind. His sandy hair fell sometimes into his eyes, which were a curious hazel color, and his body, tall like his father's, was all angles. When Robbie spoke, it was like a surprise. He never said a word about Carly's worried look, nor did he question the way she now followed him across the kitchen as he gathered another handful of birds from the sink. Standing right next to him, her hands on the counter, she pushed up on her toes and peered past his elbow into the deep sink, the water running slow and strange over the dead creatures. One by one, Robbie handled the birds, spacing them evenly across the tray. Something in the way their bodies curved slightly, the emptiness between them, seemed sad. Even so, Carly liked their calm opalescence once they'd been cleaned and laid in matching rows.

The tray's muted silver seemed as old as clouds, its metal dull and dented. It was one of Aunt Belle's old cookie sheets that had given its baking career over to the realm of the freezer—the deep freeze that hummed and murmured in a corner of the screened-in porch. Contrary to the tradition of hanging the birds by their necks to season, Aunt Belle believed in the modern methods of her Frigidaire; so she made sure Robbie knew the kitchen art of finishing the quail. Carly was taken with the way he placed their bodies—barely memories of the fat-feathered birds they'd once been—solemnly and kindly, it seemed, along the uneven surface.

"How come you line 'em up that way?" Carly asked.

"Just because," Robbie said.

"Because they fit best that way, right?" She wanted to nudge the round thigh of one bird with her fingers to line it up more evenly with the others, but she was afraid to touch them.

"I suppose so." Robbie glanced down at his cousin, then back at the tray of quail.

Carly had already grown comfortable with Robbie's lack of words, but she still asked him questions now and then. He seemed to live in a more hushed world than most boys she knew. He was an only child, just as she was, but that had only been since his older brother, Maxwell, had died over in Korea. Maybe Robbie thought about him a lot; maybe he was thinking about Maxwell right at this very minute.

Unlike the plucked chickens that Aunt Belle washed gently in the big white kitchen sink for Sunday suppers, the quail, which appeared on the table for special occasions, were minute. They had compact little bodies that huddled together in the freezer. The big yard hens were paler and cumbersome, though Aunt Belle handled them like babies. Carly grimaced at their puckered flesh, noting the indecency of the broad backsides and the broader breasts. The occasional stray feather peeked out from behind a wing, and the necks were certainly longer than they needed to be.

The quail, on the other hand, were what her mother might call "petite." The first time the men had returned with a pair of bobwhite roosters, before they'd been de-feathered, Carly had offered the wooden ruler that Aunt Belle had given her. The ruler had been meant for drawing out straight lines for pictures or math lessons, but Carly had latched on to the meaning of sizes, and lengths and widths and depths began to acquire new definitions.

Already that morning she'd measured the sides of the porch, then sat on a stool by the screen, whacking the ruler against her hand to startle the ground squirrels visiting the woodpile. She thought of how each squirrel would nearly account for the instrument's full length, while her family's yorkie would surely fall short. At breakfast she'd compared the width of her uncle's palm to the length of a postcard her father had sent from New Orleans—barely five inches. Barely five lines. The three-cent "Atoms for Peace" postage stamp was one-inch on the diagonal. Over the tight handwritten letters of her mother's name, Carly lingered but didn't tally. Her father's script spoke like a soft voice inside her head: "Vivienne, Vivienne."

Beyond the porch, the sun yellowed the yard with the parchment light of autumn, thin breaths of light that had cleared away the earlier mist and fell over the fields. In the distance the dogs were barking, the men still making their way across the meadow. Carly ran outside, waving the ruler. The first to arrive, the young dog Idle offered his long pointed snout, which was not much longer than those of the other two setters—almost four inches from their dark eyes on down. The garden's red and rose-colored zinnias reached three ruler lengths—three whole feet—while the daisies clumped together like the best and brightest eighteen inches the sun had ever seen. And out in the shed where Aunt Belle lined the nesting boxes with fresh straw every week, the chickens laid two-inch-long eggs.

The bobwhites, though, were just under ten inches each, one closer to nine; Carly wondered if one would fit in her pencil box for school. She imagined it lying inside, as silent as dust, right next to the ruler. She'd flip open the top for show-and-tell, and the girls would probably scream and carry on, as if she had just shown them a withered hand. She realized that she was fascinated with what other girls her age might think gruesome or frightening. Even so, she liked the idea of surprising her class. How everyone would know her as the girl with the dead quail in her pencil box.

* * *

Most days, since the hunting season had begun, the men went out with their guns, the dogs alongside. That afternoon, after Robbie had laid the previous day's quail on the tray and placed them on a rack inside the deep freeze, he and Uncle Theo set off. The screen door to the kitchen whined open and shut. Carly waved to the men and settled herself outside on the porch. Buttoned up in a thick flannel jacket that Robbie had given her, Carly sat at the old dinette table that lived out there year-round, kicking her legs and chewing on a pencil. She tried her best at an arithmetic problem, a scrawl of numbers on the lined page, then struggled along with yet another spelling lesson, words like "mischievous" and "adventuresome" making her mind wander.

She thought of how her father didn't enjoy hunting, but how her mother could handle a shotgun and had walked out with the men on many occasions, how she'd brought back partridges as well as quail. The men in the hunting parties all admitted Vivienne was the best shot among them, and she responded always with laughter and amused descriptions of the "unglorious ditches" and "fields of wickedly tall grasses" they'd had to traverse on those afternoons. Carly remembered little of these visits, mostly her mother's liveliness and her father's quiet, except for the time her father had stayed behind, rustling the newspaper in a loud, unhappy way and announcing to no one in particular that once again their president, dear old Dwight, was off on vacation, "golfing or hunting or some such."

Gunshots cracked open the stillness. Until recently, their echo never failed to startle her. She gazed up from the column of bold-print words in her primer and supposed how, off in the distance, Robbie and Uncle Theo were striding through the tall grass after the rustle and swish where the dogs had just run. Thelma, the older bitch, would probably lean forward and then point toward a clump of thick bracken. Quickly, an upended confusion of birds and single-barreled return. Thelma and France standing still, heads turned, awaiting their commands. Two birds down and two bird dogs searching out the kill; young Idle might even step up and nose a fallen quail.

Carly wasn't allowed on the hunt, but had sought out stories from Robbie, who offered her a few details of the pine-shaded paths they took, the bend of the grass, the sounds of quail and the dogs and even their own footsteps. So she sidled up to long moments of reverie in which she pretended to walk along with her cousin, several heads taller, her trotting to his long-legged pace. A breeze might cut through the trees, but that didn't matter, for they were downwind. They'd cross over into one more field, hoping for that last covey to fly up—tipping the grass tops with their wings and spinning against the soft still nearing of night with their high warbling cries.

These cries were different than their calls. The pitch of alarm was quick and panicked, and the particular slant of movement at this point always became chaotic. Carly believed this as so because this sound needed to be completely different than the sound of the quail she'd become familiar with. Often, in the early mornings, when she lay still in the warmth of the bed covers, Carly listened to the bobwhite quail call out their own names: "bob-white, bob-bob-white." Boy quail and girl quail and mama and daddy quail. Morning murmurings of a family. "Hoy... koi-lee... bob-white." Bright, feathery mimics of the younger generations and the lulled response of the grown-ups. Carly snuggled inside her happy bird thoughts, content that the quail were so much like family, that they lived together and cared about each other, just like Aunt Belle and Uncle Theo cared for her, just like she looked up to Robbie at the edge of each day.

Sent upstairs that evening for her bath, Carly walked slowly to the bathroom, holding a sleeve of her nightgown and allowing its hem to brush the floor. In the hallway at the head of the stairs, family photos lined the wall. Carly lingered under the sconce lamps, their dim light scarcely brightening the faces in the photographs. Aunt Belle in a wedding dress looking off into the woods. Robbie as a baby with round cheeks and hardly any hair. Uncle Theo and a young boy with dark hair and dark eyes, holding up a string of fish, sunlight bright on their silvery sides. Her father. Her mother. Young and childless. Composed faces opening out to the camera's lens, looking out from the wooden frame. Carly reached up to her mother's face. It seemed pale and unknowing; it seemed like someone else's face.

Carly began to hum a song her mother liked. Something about a wildwood flower. Opposite the bathroom door, there was another set of photos. A baby and a boy in short trousers. Two boys at their aunt and uncle's wedding. Several more revealed clusters of people: a christening, grandparents playing croquet on a back lawn, cousins grown and gone off to places like Biloxi and Grand Isle. Carly remembered her family's recent vacation on the Gulf. The warm sand, the sound of the water, her father's voice. "Vivienne, darlin', are you all right?" They'd thought she was sleeping under the sun umbrella. Carly supposed her mother slept all the time now, the dim light of autumn behind pulled blinds.

Though the memories were faint, Carly recalled her mother in Mississippi only months before as alive and bright, like another person altogether. Color rose in her cheeks and her laughter broke the mornings into sunny-side-up moments. In New Orleans she became more languid, letting others do for her, waving at the unkempt weeds in their garden that eventually bloomed into white and lavender lace, the word "unglorious" on her lips, a word that before had been attached to happiness and high spirits.

Down past the linen closet, there was a pair of photographs. One of

Robbie at Carly's age, or so she guessed, holding a shotgun and a thick handful of killed bobwhite. Just behind stood a taller boy, certainly Maxwell. Maxwell was very tall, and his face was glad, his eyes squinting heavily, his broad mouth in a smile. But Robbie seemed tired somehow. Carly put her thumb across his face to cover it, and when she took her thumb away, she found his expression undone, distraught, a stamped-down version of sadness.

"That was my first hunt."

Carly turned around. Robbie stood in his bedroom doorway. She'd wandered clear down to the end of the hall. Clear down to Robbie's room. Startled, not wanting to be caught studying this particular photo, she avoided his glance.

"I missed everything I aimed at."

Carly looked past Robbie to the very end of the hall, only steps away. There was the window seat and the window that looked out onto the fields and farther away into the woods. But it was night now, and only darkness colored the glass. Black and still, without curtains to crowd the starless view.

"Maxwell shot my birds that day."

Carly gathered her nightgown as it began to fall, the thin cotton wrinkling as she twisted its sleeves together. "He did?"

"Yes," said Robbie. "That day and every day after that until he left."

There were no photographs of Maxwell in uniform.

"They sent him home only weeks after he shipped out."

Carly stepped back and her heel touched the molding where floor and wall met. She lost her balance for a second and, trying to catch herself, instead caught the corner of a small frame with her elbow. It tipped and hung at an angle. Maxwell and two setters stared out, out of kilter, swinging. Robbie walked over and righted the picture.

"He never even got to see his dogs again." He looked down at Carly. "Do you know he taught them everything? Everything they didn't know by instinct, that is."

"He never met Idle then?"

Robbie shook his head, his hair shading one side of his face, and pressed his lips together. "No," he said. "He didn't."

They didn't get to talk anymore that night, once Aunt Belle had called up the stairs, asking Carly if she'd finished her bath. And so then she'd had to go on and take it. But later, gradually, as they spent time together, Robbie told Carly more about his brother: how Maxwell had watched over him with the strictness of a father, how his mother seemed to love Max as if he were the only son, how his father had to work longer days after Robbie had come along, another boy to raise.

Carly liked to sit in the window seat outside Robbie's bedroom and read to herself or watch out the window or stare at the photographs on the wall above. The wallpaper was a repeated pattern of trumpet vines, which seemed to clutch the backs of the frames and hold them in place. The photos of Maxwell revealed the progression of boy to man; he had a smile that dazzled, and Carly could understand why her aunt had been so smitten with her eldest. Robbie's likeness seemed soiled by discontent or some sort of unexplained undoing. He didn't smile; his eyes wide and knowing, he did not smile.

One afternoon Robbie came out of his room and sat down next to his cousin.

"You shouldn't sit here," he said.

"I like to sit here." She closed her book. "You shouldn't tell me what to do."

"I know you're looking at him and wondering all about him. He's not so special. Everyone always said he was the special one, but he's not. He's just dead."

"Are you mad at him?" Carly felt her brow begin to furrow. "How in the world can you be mad at someone who's dead?"

Sunlight cut through the window, glancing Robbie's shoulders, the back of his head, the cover of Carly's book, and then just as quickly dimmed behind a shawl of clouds.

"The idea of him is still around," Robbie said, his voice stretched from here to there. "You can tell that. That's why you're sitting here." His palm came down on the seat cushion. "All he is now is a three-cornered American flag folded up tight and some pictures on the wall. That's all."

Carly bit her lip and looked out the window. "I think you're mad 'cause he never came home."

Robbie sat silent. The day outside was warm for early December. Inside, the air was still.

"In the fall," Robbie said, "when it's time to hunt, I can finally go on and do it. Without his hand on my shoulder, his breath on my neck. Without him telling me what to do, how to aim, when to fire."

"You couldn't before?" Carly felt truly puzzled. "Why didn't you just tell him to let you alone?"

"I did," Robbie said. "He always said I did it all wrong. That's what brothers do. They tell you how you do everything all wrong."

"Well, I'm glad I don't have one then," Carly said and thought a minute. "A sister wouldn't be much better."

"It would depend on the sister." Robbie smiled at Carly. "If she liked autumn; if she didn't mind the smell of dogs, or the look of dead birds, or the sound of a shotgun firing; if she knew how to hush and when to laugh and—"

"And when to cry?" Carly said. "But boys don't do that, do they?"

Carly wondered if Robbie knew it would be okay to cry. She wondered if he thought about what it might have been like for Maxwell so far from home. She wondered if she would eventually be angry with her mother because her mother was sure to leave her alone just like Maxwell had gone and left Robbie alone. She was sure she would be, but right now that feeling was just an idea, curled up and sleeping, small and inelegant, like a downed quail.

One Thursday afternoon, when the wind hardly whispered and the sky had an ashen color to it, Robbie went out alone on a hunt. Uncle Theo arrived home late in the evenings now from the newspaper office in town. It was getting close to Christmas, and he had things to finish up before the holidays set in. Carly sat at the kitchen table with a plate of gingersnaps and a jelly glass of milk. She noticed Aunt Belle's even expression when Robbie gathered up the shells and his twenty-gauge from the rack by the back door. France was impatient to go and barked until Robbie told him to settle down. Thelma already waited outside, but Idle stayed under Carly's swinging feet even when the door opened. Robbie stood in the door, waiting for the third dog, then said to Carly, "You watch him, okay? He doesn't need to come." Carly nodded at her cousin, glad finally to be responsible for something besides homework. Idle nosed her ankles, and she dropped bits of cookie past her knees when her aunt wasn't looking.

"You like dogs, don't you?" Aunt Belle said. She didn't turn around from the counter where she worked, as usual busy and competent, cutting thick pieces of beef into smaller ones. She had a habit of talking to her family while facing away from them. Probably so as to keep up with her tasks, Carly thought.

"Yes, ma'am," Carly said. "We have a dog at home."

"That's right." Aunt Belle put the knife down and looked over her shoulder for a second. Her auburn hair softened her face, which always had a look that Carly thought of as sensible. "Some sort of terrier, isn't it?"

"He's a yorkie, and he's really Mama's dog. Why, he'd sit in her lap all day—" Carly gazed across the table—the milk glass blurring, the checked tablecloth a whirl of patterned color. Her mother had been moved to another ward in the hospital that week. The doctors were not hopeful.

"What's his name again?" Aunt Belle's words were weighted like spoonfuls of sugar—just enough, not too much, not too sweet. She was thoughtful about silence but never let it lie about too long in her bright kitchen.

"Well, his fancy name is Étienne, but Mama's always called him Cushion." Carly nudged her socked foot against Idle, who seemed unconcerned about the mound of meat hulking up on the counter.

"Cushion? Whatever for?" Aunt Belle said. There was nearly a ring to her voice.

"'Cause he acts like Mama's his," Carly said. "His cushion. But then she turned it all around, and now he's her Cushion. Mama does that. Turns things around." Carly wondered if her mother could turn time around, reverse the rheumatic fever she'd had as a child; if she could bust down the hospital doors; if her heart would swell up and burst with joy.

"Your mama's a kick, that's for sure," Aunt Belle said, loading handfuls of the meat into a large black skillet.

Idle raised his head for a moment, then rested it against Carly.

"Yeah," Carly said. "Everyone says that about Mama. How funny she is. She says I'm quirky, just like her. But I don't feel that way anymore."

"I know, honey," Aunt Belle said. "I know just how you feel."

She washed her hands in the sink and dried them across the cloth of her apron. Pulling out the chair next to Carly, she sat for a moment. Her hand reached out for Carly's, which Carly knew was sticky from the cookies she'd eaten, but her aunt didn't seem to mind. On the stove the meat sizzled and rich smells filled the room. Frail light fell through the kitchen window, and Aunt Belle sighed. "I know just how you feel."

Then she patted the back of Carly's hand and stood up. "Why don't you go out after a bit and wait for Robbie? He likes it when you look out for him in the evenings." She smiled. "He wouldn't ever admit it, but he does."

"All right," Carly said. "I'll sit in the lawn chair and be real still. Sometimes, if I'm quiet, the deer come by. And then Robbie comes too."

"Well, go on then." Aunt Belle pulled out Carly's chair and tipped it slightly as if she were emptying its contents. Carly slid off with Idle following her, and she remembered to catch the screen door before it slammed.

The day had become golden, that glowing time before sunset, and a few flies circled around Idle. He snapped at them, and eventually they flew off in another direction. Carly sat down in one of the lawn chairs beside the woodpile. The chair's webbing scratched the back of her thighs. She tried to sit calmly, but instead stood up and spun in circles in the tall yellowing grass. She picked up a stick and threw it for the dog to chase. He obliged her for a few throws, then settled down to chew on the hard-to-reach area just above his tail. Carly ran her fingers over his back and helped scratch at the spot. His fur was long and whiskered, the color of timber, tangled with tiny brambles, fat little burrs, and a single dead leaf.

Robbie's figure was off in the distance, the other dogs walking close beside him, like low shadows sprung out of the stubbly grass. With his shotgun slung over his shoulder, her cousin looked more like a grown man than a boy. But his movements weren't as deliberate as his father's, and the way he reached down and batted at the setters revealed his youthfulness. Despite his mild demeanor, he had another side that showed when he stopped thinking so hard. At least, Carly trusted this as so. When his eyes lit up and his shoulders relaxed, he'd say just about anything and seemed happy doing so.

She watched him walk back now, past the tree line of tall longleaf pines, across the back meadow and straight over to the woodpile. At first, she thought he would empty his pockets, but instead, he motioned for her to join him. She ran, legs pumping, over the back lawn, with Idle out in front. The three setter dogs bumped up against each other, and Thelma gave a sharp bark.

From his worn cotton vest, Robbie pulled out something surprising, completely enclosed inside his hand, and held it out to Carly. Resting in his curved palm was a small speckled egg, much smaller than a chicken's egg. Set there, just so, like an undiscovered Easter treat.

"Is it a quail's egg?" Carly said.

"Yes," Robbie said. "I found it under a patch of briar near the alfalfa field. It was still in a nest, but I let that alone." He let it circle around in his cupped hand. "I'd just taken down a couple of bob and was following France. He likes to brush up against the kill before he retrieves, and he found the nest along the way." He looked down at the egg. "Little, isn't it?"

"It's tiny," Carly said. "Will it hatch without its mama?"

"No, it's long past nesting season." He held the egg down to Carly. "You want it?"

"I suppose," Carly said. "I suppose I could take it for show-and-tell." She imagined it rolling around in her pencil box. She would have to wrap it up, so it wouldn't break. The egg felt light and hollow. She thought about shaking it and then changed her mind.

"Here," Robbie said, holding out a quail. "I'll teach you how to clean them."

All too quickly, Carly had an egg in one hand and a lifeless quail in the other. She thought the sky shifted a bit at that moment, and then realized she was dizzy.

"Sit down here," Robbie told her.

She sat on the lawn chair and looked down at her hands, which still held the egg and the quail. The shell and the feathers had similar colors: dusky browns and grays with cream and dots of black mixed in. Uncertain of what to do next, she glanced up at Robbie.

"Just put the egg in your shirt pocket," he said, "and then you'll have both hands to work with."

"Okay," Carly said, trying to remember where her pocket was located. Oh, right there. Over her heart. Her heart, sending out tiny rhythms. Her mother's heart, trying to expand and contract and carry on. The bobwhite's heart, no longer beating.

"Watch me first. Then you can try, okay?"

Carly nodded. She felt the texture of the quail's feathers against her hand and against her legs as it lay in her lap. As the sun settled closer to the treetops, the air became cool.

Robbie sat in the chair next to Carly and pulled out his hunting knife. With a deft draw of the blade against the slim throat, he quickly beheaded the small bird. It was as if he drew a line over the black feather necklace that ringed the neck, as if separating a head from a body were a quaint, everyday affair. He then slid the knife under the feathers at the neck and at the tail and pulled the skin and plumage off in two neat movements. Next went the feet, and then he laid down the knife. There were smells—loamy and dank, then sharp and bitter. The dogs sat up now. Robbie reached inside the bird.

"The heart, the moon, the stars and clovers," he said to Carly and grinned a little.

He dropped them into the tin bowl, and Carly stared at the dark pink insides as the setters waited expectantly. Robbie placed the cleaned bird onto the stump by the woodpile. Carly held out the feathered bobwhite that she'd had in her lap. Its head leaned to one side, limp. Its belly and tail felt fat and heavy. The feathers followed a pattern—rows of Vs all lined up, one after the other, in varying shades of brown and darker brown and nibs of cream and threads of black. It reminded Carly of the herringbone jacket her mother wore every autumn. But her mother's jacket had grown coarse with wear over the years, and the quail's coat was still new, fine and delicate and just a bit damp.

Carly considered the dogs, how carefully they carried the fallen quail. "Does France have a gentle mouth?" she asked.

"Yes, he does. See where he roughed up this one's cap though?"

The bobwhite's black-brown head feathers tufted up in a comical way.

"You take it," Carly said. "I'm afraid I'll mess up my clothes."

"You sure?"

"I'll just watch again."

"All right then." Robbie took the bird. And everything went on as before, ending in "the heart and the stars and the moon and little clovers."

On Sunday they drove to church in Uncle Theo's Plymouth. Carly thought its worn, two-toned chassis was nearly the color of the caramel cake with thick cream frosting that Aunt Belle had made for supper the night before. It was raining, so they drove slowly on a back road into town. The car's interior was wide and smelled of aged, cracked leather. Carly splayed her fingers on either side of her brown gingham dress as the car traveled the rough road. Robbie stared out of his own rain-splattered window.

The day had taken on the gray narrow confines of winter. It wasn't as if, by driving to church, by singing hymns and slipping their hands between prayer book pages, they would change anything. Aunt Belle had taken charge of things and decided that they should simply move through the day's usual rhythms.

Carly understood the words that morning, words that thudded softly around her and her nearly empty breakfast plate. They ate griddlecakes and thick smoked bacon, and Carly was allowed to cover her entire plate in swarms of maple syrup. The usual clatter of dishes and chairs pushing back at meal's end didn't happen though. Instead, Aunt Belle lingered longer at the table, and Uncle Theo cleared his throat several times. Robbie gazed at the dogs, lying like enormous panting rugs across the kitchen floor.

"Carly," Aunt Belle said.

"Yes, ma'am?"

"Carly, your father called this morning." Aunt Belle's eyes had a depth to them Carly didn't remember noticing before. "It was very early."

"I heard the phone ring," Carly said quietly. She rested her fork against the few uneaten bites, now growing cold. "I saw out the window it was raining."

"Yes, sweetheart, it was already raining." Aunt Belle stopped for a moment and folded her hands in her lap. "Your daddy said your mama left us last night, that her heart just couldn't go on. And, you know, honey, it had gone on for so much longer than anyone ever expected."

Aunt Belle cried then, right there at the table. Uncle Theo reached over to Carly, touching her shoulder, and promised to drive to New Orleans, all of them together, the following morning. And in the meantime, there was church to attend and the day ahead to remember their wonderful Vivienne. Aunt Belle nodded in agreement and pulled a handkerchief from her pocket. She'd prepare a supper in Vivienne's honor, a supper of roasted quail with pan gravy and red-skinned potatoes and wild mushrooms and autumn greens and baked apples drizzled with cream and caramelized sugar. And at bedtime they would tuck Carly into warm blankets.

Carly imagined her mother tucking her in, how she'd fall asleep, the late autumn calls of the bobwhites in her mind, and in the morning wake up in her own bed, her daddy standing there, saying those familiar words, "O Best Beloved," everything just fine.

While his parents spoke, Robbie stayed silent but continued to look from Carly to the dogs and back again. Eventually, Uncle Theo teared up, and Aunt Belle finished by telling Carly how brave and beautiful her mother would always be, now that she was up in heaven. Carly hadn't cried. She'd thanked Aunt Belle for breakfast and even tugged on Uncle Theo's sleeve. She looked at Robbie out of the corner of her eyes and went out on the porch. The morning was thick with mist. She waited and listened. Nothing stirred. Even the bobwhites were still sleeping.

And now in the car, it was quiet. Carly was glad for the sound of the car's engine, for the rush and wash of the rainwater beneath the tires. The woods blurred on and on, and the ditch beside the road heaved along, damp and unglorious. Then she saw one. Outside her window nearly hidden in the tall grass was a lone quail.

"Stop!" she said.

Uncle Theo swerved, and Aunt Belle shouted for him to be careful. He slowed the car and pulled over.

"What's wrong, child?" Aunt Belle said, turning around with a troubled look on her face.

Carly pushed open the car door. It swung wide, and the car shuddered. Carly jumped down onto the roadside gravel.

"Carly?" Uncle Theo's voice was taut.

Back a ways the quail hovered in the wet ditchgrass. Carly stood beside the car while the rain continued its steady course.

"Carly, hon, get back into the car," Aunt Belle said. "Theo? There she goes. Theo."

Carly walked toward the hollowed-out place where an old fence had become covered in hedge. Just below sat the bobwhite quail, looking wet and sullen. As she approached, the bird flattened itself. She squatted down, very close now, the brome sedge and weeds grazing her legs, and considered picking up the cross little thing. Its wings were spread, revealing the tawny brown and white stripes, the shy grays and sharper tones of black, the configuration that made the bird disappear into its background.

Robbie stood next to her. With a movement like breath, fine and controlled, he lifted the quail, one hand over its back, the other under its breast, and held it out to Carly. The bobwhite blinked at her. The band of black feathers across his eyes gave him the face of a bandit. She had known this before, but all the birds before this one had had closed eyes and blank faces. She recognized this blinking look as one of fright and, strangely, of acceptance. She stroked the crown of its head with one finger.

"We should let it go," she said to Robbie.

"You're sure?" he asked now as he had only days before. He tilted the quail, and it folded its wings.

"Yes, I'm sure." Carly hesitated, and in her hesitation, something shifted and then in the slightest way adjusted itself. She looked hard at Robbie. "If we let it go, it'll be all right again."

Carly heard a car door open and turned to see her aunt standing on the roadside, her white-gloved hands held open to the raindrops.

"Carly, please," said Aunt Belle.

Carly stared at her aunt for a moment. She looked sad and distressed, and Carly knew this was her fault. The rain kept coming down.

Turning back to her cousin, Carly reached out. She touched the bob-white's throat and felt it quiver. There was something in its response, brave and sudden and disquieting. And still, standing there on the side of the road in the rain, she didn't cry.

"Let him go," she said.

Hands outstretched, Robbie tossed the small bird gently over the hedge-row towards a tangled thicket of saplings and wild blackberry vines. It flew for a moment and settled out of view, as if it had never been there.

Some months later, when the meaning of her mother's death had settled in her mind—in the way she'd stand in front of her mother's dresser, the big mirror reflecting her straight shoulders, her dark shoulder-length hair, her wide-set hazel eyes, so like her mother's—Carly understood there had been a color to that Sunday morning in Picayune, Mississippi. She considered its twist and texture, how it wrapped itself around her thoughts, how she'd daydream in the midst of company who came with condolences. The brief encounter with the little bobwhite was a moment she relived over and over. Just as she was afraid of losing the memory of her mother's laughter and the way her sentences lingered at the end, like questions, Carly also feared the possibility of forgetting the bobwhites' morning calls—how they'd comfort-ed her when she'd felt so unsure.

In the china saucer that held her mother's jewelry—stray earrings, a strand of pearls without a clasp—the little quail egg lay. The one that Robbie had given her. Tiny and rare and round. Creamy browns dotted with flecks the color of cocoa. Its speckled hue brightened the memory of that morning so close to Christmas, the morning that one heart failed while another flew, both leaving for thickets, dense and wild and mysterious.

ACKNOWLEDGMENTS

I am thrilled that *The Geography of First Kisses* is making her way into the world. There are so many brilliant people to thank for sending these stories toward the prize-winning collection they've become. Right at the start, I'd like to thank those who are holding the book in their hands—the readers. Here's hoping that the compass points and little miracles of these stories take you places you've never been and leave you laughing and perhaps sighing and thinking for a long while after you read them.

Please deliver a round of applause and a case of champagne directly to Valerie Borchardt, my agent, who always assures me with her calm attention and incredible wit and her confident way of navigating the literary world. Thank you, Georges Borchardt, for loving the book's title. And, yes, I do believe there is a map.

Sincere gratitude to Tony Burnett, Executive Director of Kallisto Gaia Press, for recognizing these stories as worthy of the Acacia Fiction Prize and for your patience, guidance, and kindness. Amazing thanks to the team of KGP editors who sent this collection upward toward the award and publication. To Jan Rider Newman, the rarest of editors, my utmost thanks for your insight, knowledge, and generosity and for your love of all things Louisiana.

Infinite appreciation to artist, Annie Russell, whose gorgeous illustration and cover design beautifully reflect the timbre and sway of the stories. You are so talented, and I am beyond lucky to know you. And to graphic designer, Savannah Adams, a thousand thanks for saving the day.

To the teachers who led me toward more nuance and drive and understanding in many of these stories, I owe enormous gratitude—Laurie Foos, Margot

Livesey, Erin McGraw, Kyoko Mori, Daniel Mueller, and A.J. Verdelle. Thank you for your observational wisdom and honesty, your encouragement and humor.

Love and thanks to my community of fellow writers for responding to these pieces in their earliest drafts—Bruce Alexander, Seth Borgen, Mark Edwards, Alicia Hyland, Hayley Krischer, Chaney Kwak, Jessica Lawrence, Lyz Lenz, Brian Liddy, Kelly Magee, Katherine Mariaca-Sullivan, and Lauren Inness Norton.

A Room of Her Own Foundation allowed me to experience firsthand the support of women writers by women in the literary arts world. I am still in awe of the fine work AROHO has accomplished over the years. My utmost thanks to Breena Clarke for selecting "The Geography of First Kisses" as the winner of AROHO's Orlando Prize for Short Fiction. With this same generosity in mind, I'm ever grateful to *Passages North* and guest judge Caitlin Horrocks, who chose "We Are Here Because of a Horse" as the winner of the Waasmode Short Fiction Prize.

Endless appreciation to the Sewanee Writers' Conference, Lesley University MFA in Creative Writing Program, and the Greater Columbus Arts Council for their generous support in a multitude of ways, many of them extraordinary, including the gifts of community, direction, and funding.

Over the years these stories have appeared in many literary reviews, and I'd like to thank their devoted and hardworking editors: Kelly Davio at *The Los Angeles Review of Books*; Tim Johnston of *Passages North*; Lindy Dentinger at *New Delta Review*; Josh Collins at *Newfound*; Katherine Conner at *Gris-Gris Journal*; Michael Nye at *Story Magazine*; Cliff Garstang at *Prime Number Magazine*; Sarah Cedeño at *Animal Literary Review*; Christopher Boucher at *Post Road*, along with Guest Folio Editor Elizabeth Graver; Emily Wojcik at *The Massachusetts Review*; Tyler Yearling Hively at *Filigree Literary Magazine*; John Henry Fleming and Gloria Muñoz at *Saw Palm*; and Megan Sexton at *Five Points*.

To my dear friends and family, y'all are the best! Shout-outs to Mama, Anne, Liz, Brad, Lacey, and Barbara for being so supportive and inspiring and crazy and adventurous and fun. Sending celebratory dancing-in-place images and loud thankful laughter straight over to Hannah and Zak in return for all their love and nonsense. And once across an ocean, but now just across the room, a final toss of thanks—always-and-forever thanks—to John.

CPSIA information can be obtained
at www.ICGtesting.com
Printed in the USA
JSHW082324020423
39815JS00004B/25